Blackjacks & Blue Devils

FIRST EDITION, 2011

Blackjacks & Blue Devils
© 2011 Jerry Wilson

ISBN 978-0-9833052-5-5

Cover Image:
©Jim Howell 2011

MONGREL EMPIRE PRESS
NORMAN, OK

ONLINE CATALOGUE: WWW.MONGRELEMPIRE.ORG

This publisher is a proud member of

Book Design: Mongrel Empire Press using iWork Pages

Blackjacks and Blue Devils

By

Jerry Wilson

MONGREL EMPIRE PRESS
NORMAN, OKLAHOMA, UNITED STATES OF AMERICA

2011

Acknowledgments

Versions of the following stories were previously published in these magazines and journals:

"A Change of Worlds," Sioux City, IA: *Briar Cliff Review*, Spring, 1993.

"Desire and Shifting Sand," Mitchell, SD: *Prairie Winds*, Spring, 1993.

"Moonlighting." Mitchell, SD: *Prairie Winds*, Spring, 1990.

"That Old Time Religion." Tahlequah, OK: *Phoenix*, Spring, 1990.

"Over the Hill." Brownsville, TX and Cedar Falls, IA: University of Texas and University of Northern Iowa, *Short Story*, Spring, 1996.

"The Ends of the Earth." Yankton, SD: *Midstream*, Spring, 1990.

CONTENTS

DUST

She looked tiny in the big iron bed. Could this be the woman who'd guided a horse-drawn plow, busting sod to plant wheat? The first white child born on Cheyenne-Arapaho land after the run of 1892, born in a dugout with a wagon-cover roof? Paper-thin lids hid the fiery eyes that had commanded Adrian's obedience as a child. Her breathing was slow but peaceful, her gnarled hands crossed over the patchwork quilt that had kept him warm the winter she nursed him through chicken pox.

Adrian's finger traced the bulging vein from bony knuckles to wrist. The skin was cold and dry. But could she really die? He took her hand in his and squeezed it, as if to press his warmth and life into its limpness. "Grandma," he whispered near her ear, "Grandma." The eyes opened, not a flame but a feeble flicker.

"Adrian, you've come," she said. The slightest of smiles creased her parched lips. "You've come to let me die." Her voice was both wavering and strong.

"No Grandma," Adrian said. "I've come to spend Christmas with you, just like always."

Her lips parted in a faint chuckle. "Let's not pretend," she mumbled. "Now that everybody's here, I can die in peace." Adrian felt a faint squeeze of her hand. Her legs quivered under the quilt. "Just sit with me awhile and I'll rest." The blue lids closed.

Through the bedroom window Adrian could barely make out the barn. Gusts whipped dust and snow across the yard and into a graceful arc around the lonely elm. It was Christmas Eve, and he'd planned to come anyway, but his sister Jane had called after midnight to say Grandma was slipping fast; he should come soon if he wanted to see her alive. He was well beyond Oklahoma City when the sun rose clear, but the radio promised a blizzard for the Panhandle. The northwest sky was ominous and dark when he stopped for breakfast in Watonga; the rest of the trip was into the teeth of the storm.

Highway 3 roughly followed the route his grandparents had taken when they moved west, nearly seventy years before. The road was dirt then, little more than a cattle trail. The trip by wagon had taken a week. Now the road ran smooth and straight through swirling flakes that softened the unrelenting flatness of plowed wheat ground.

It was well past noon when Adrian hit Boise City, the last town in the Panhandle, and he was hungry. He considered stopping for lunch, but he knew Aunt Ruby would have something to eat. Jane's words, "Grandma is dying," replayed in his head, and he pushed on, the last fifteen miles across wheat stubble and turned earth and blowing dust and snow, with now and then a derelict fence or gaping barn to break the monotony.

There were other cars at the end of the long driveway; aunts and uncles and cousins were here. Jane embraced him at the door. "I'm glad you're here," she said. "I don't know how much longer she'll last."

Jane rushed him through hellos and hugs and into Grandma's room. The bed, her wedding present from her folks, nearly filled the room. In this bed her children were conceived and born. The iron frame had ridden to the Panhandle lashed between the wagon side and the coops that held a dozen laying hens. "We'd have starved if we hadn't brought those hens," Grandma always said. "The neighbors advised us to sell them in Okeene, said they'd never last a week on the trail." She looked at peace in the big featherbed.

A blast of wind rattled the window, and Adrian gazed at the swaybacked barn, which appeared and disappeared in the blowing snow. The elm beside the barn was stripped of leaves. A Russian thistle skipped and danced across the yard, drove against the house and stuck. It was mid-afternoon, but the sky was like dusk. What light the one small window admitted could not dispel the gloom, but once his eyes adjusted, memory supplied details.

The wallpaper was the same as when he'd lain sick in that bed, how long ago? Thirty years? No, forty or more. The same lavender-flowered paper that Grandma had hung with flour paste. The dresser was crowded with small framed pictures of the family, the children and grandchildren and great-grandchildren whose mingled voices now registered a low murmur through the bedroom door. The largest picture was of Grandpa. Beside the bed was the family Bible, all the births and weddings and deaths carefully recorded in the tattered front page. How many times had Adrian read that page?

The most remarkable thing about the room was the pictures that hung on every wall, cheap landscape prints of the kind one can buy in any variety store. There was a scene in the Florida Everglades, which Grandpa and Grandma visited when Uncle Herb was there in the Navy in 1942. On another wall was a rushing river, water cascading in white foam across the rocks. Over the bed was a placid lake somewhere in the mountains, probably Colorado, where Grandma loved to go. The fourth was an ocean scene, big waves breaking on a vast sandy shore. Grandma always did love water, Adrian remembered. Strange she spent most of her life in a place where there was no water in sight, where between scarce rains the only water was a hundred feet below hard-packed earth.

Adrian settled back in the squeaking rocking chair and straightened the doilies Grandma had crocheted. The wind rattled the window again, and the tumbleweed broke loose, bouncing on toward Texas. He wondered if there were still enough fences left in this desolate country to stop its tumble somewhere in the Panhandle where, like Grandma, it had grown old. Snow swirled past the house, but it was warm in the little room. Adrian felt the weariness of the short night and the long drive, and closed his eyes.

"Adrian." It was Jane, gently shaking him. "Come and have a little supper. Aunt Edith will sit with Grandma now." Adrian opened his eyes to the lavender grey of dusty twilight. Grandma's breathing was labored but regular. He looked a long moment at her sun- and wind-creased face, now lighted by a dim lamp beside the chair. He followed Jane to the bright steamy kitchen.

Conversation was subdued. The kids were in the living room, gathered around the little cedar Christmas tree Uncle Herb had cut on Black Mesa. The rest of the family hovered around the stove or the table, nibbling leftovers from the noon meal. Adrian smelled turkey dressing and remembered he hadn't eaten since morning. He helped himself to a plateful, the only one not too stuffed to still appreciate Aunt Ruby's cooking.

The doctor had been there in the morning. Grandma's blood pressure was so low he was surprised she was conscious and alert. "She's no ordinary woman," Aunt Edna had reminded him. The family had watched Grandma pull through more than one crisis, and everybody wanted to believe she could do it again.

"But she is eighty-eight," Herb reminded them. "She can't last forever."

After supper the older folks joined the kids for awhile in the living room, but there was little that hadn't been said. About nine Herb and Edith got up to go home, and others began to stir. They'd all taken their turns by Grandma's bed over a couple of weeks. The food was put away and everybody except Jane and Adrian found their coats. The men went out to start the cars, and a few minutes later the others headed into the howling darkness to drive to Herb and Edith's big house in town.

"I can sit with her tonight," Jane said when they were gone. "You must be exhausted. Why don't you go on to bed for awhile?"

"Thanks," Adrian said, "I'm O.K. I want to be with her. You get some rest. If I need you I'll wake you." Jane kissed him and said good night. Adrian had a last cup of coffee and went back to Grandma's room.

He saw immediately that her breathing had changed. A hollow rattle shook her throat, and every breath seemed a demanding chore. Her brow was sweaty and hot, and Adrian wiped it dry. Then she opened her eyes, and they were searching and wild.

"Andrew!" she said in a gravelly voice, "You're here. Now we can start. The wagon's all loaded and the kids are ready. The canned fruit is packed under the mattresses. I think it'll ride there, don't you? Everybody's here to send us off, and they say they'll come to see us. Time to go, Andrew. I'll get the kids in the wagon. Better check old Council's left-rear hoof. He's favoring it some. Children, say goodbye." Her hand fluttered feebly, as if to wave. "It'll be a long time before we see our folks again. Time to say goodbye." Grandma's voice trailed off, and tears pooled in her pale eyes.

"Grandma, it's me," Adrian said, taking her hand and bending close to her weathered face. The purple mole on her cheek was the same as when he was a child.

Her faded eyes searched his for a long moment. "Why, of course, Adrian," she said. "Of course I know you. I'm so glad you're here. I was waiting 'til everybody came so we could start. It's going to be a long trip. I just hope it won't be too hot for the hens. I sure wouldn't want to lose my layers. Be sure we have plenty of water, dear. Are the milk cans full? You know, Adrian, what I think I'll miss most is the spring. I don't believe there's water as sweet and cold as Spring Creek anywhere else in the world."

"Grandma, I'm your grandson, Adrian," he persisted, alarmed by the galloping range of her mind. "Is there anything I can get you, Grandma?"

Her eyes narrowed, and she stared hard into his. He smelled death in her rasping breath, and recoiled. But her eyes held him, and her cracked lips began to tremble. "Yes," she said at last. "Could you bring me a drink of water?"

Adrian brought a glass of water from the kitchen sink and raised her up to drink. She swallowed hard, and a little dribbled from the corner of her mouth onto her nightgown. She was so light he wondered for an instant if she was already gone, if he held but her spirit in his arms. She swallowed again and choked a little, and Adrian took the glass away. "Thank you," she said. "It seems I just can't get enough water since the well went dry."

"Grandma, I just got this water from the kitchen faucet," he told her. "The well is fine. Good cold water too, isn't it?"

A spark returned to her pallid eyes. "It all started with Hoover," she said. "We were doing fine 'til he got elected. Why in '26 we raised thirty-bushel wheat. Did you know that boy? Thirty bushels an acre and nearly two dollars a bushel. That's how we built this house, you know. 1927." I guess you wouldn't remember that, would you?"

"No, Grandma," Adrian chuckled. "That was a little before my time."

"Yes, it all started with Hoover," she said again, and the spark flared to fire. "Twenty-three cents a bushel, and it cost that much to grow it. I guess that was what really got Grandpa down. And then the wind, and the dust. Always the dust. Dust an inch thick in this very room. Dust in the food. Eyes full of dust. Dust in the bed, between bodies. Having babies in the dust. Hens dying right and left, choked by dust. It was awful. Believe me, boy, we knew plenty of blue devils in those years. And it all started with Hoover." Her legs strained under the quilt, trying to raise her body up. Anger flushed her wrinkled cheeks. Her hoarse, cracking voice became a gasping cough.

"Easy, Grandma," Adrian said. "Just take it easy." He encircled her in his arms and hugged her slender shoulders for awhile, then eased her back onto the pillow. "You'd better rest awhile, Grandma."

She closed her eyes, but only for a minute, and when they opened they were wild again. She seemed to look right through him at something else.

"Didn't you find him, Andrew?" she demanded. "If you can't find him, I'm going out there myself. I don't care what it's like. Wet that handkerchief for me. My boy's out there somewhere, and I'm going to find him. Now get out of my way." Her arm pulled free of the quilt and flailed feebly across her breast. "The dust's so thick out there I can't even see the barn. It's black as night and he's lost out there, and I'm going out to get him. Now let go of me, Andrew!"

Grandma's voice had risen to a croaking shout. Every worn-out muscle was straining to raise her body out of bed, but the quilt held her down. She wrenched sideways and turned her gray head to the window. "You see how dark it is out there, Andrew. I've got to go find him!"

"There now, Grandma," Adrian said, his arms around her again, gently holding her struggling body until it was calm. "Sure it's dark out there. It's Christmas Eve, and we've all come to spend Christmas with you."

Her eyes searched, and then it seemed that she saw him again. "What time is it, Adrian?" she asked. He looked at his watch.

"It's almost midnight," he answered. "It's ten minutes to twelve."

"So it's almost Christmas then?" She seemed to relax, to be at peace. "We made it, didn't we? And everybody's here to see us off."

She was still for a time except for the harsh irregular breathing, which now seemed to draw in pain with every breath. Then she turned her head again. "Adrian, there's something I want you to do."

"Of course, Grandma. What is it?"

"First, a little drink of water," she said. He raised her once more and put the glass to her parched lips. She took a gurgling swallow, then moved her lips away. "Now. In the attic is a trunk, you may remember. There is a diary, a diary I kept when I was a young woman, starting . . . before everything happened. Bring it to me." Her hand crept slowly from the quilt again and raised trembling, her smooth cold fingers touching his cheek. A little smile arched her lips. Adrian bent and kissed her burning brow.

He found a flashlight in a cabinet drawer and climbed to the attic. He hardly needed a light to find the trunk he remembered well. It contained countless treasures he had wondered over as a boy. Ancient yellow letters in funny formal-looking handwriting. Uncle Herb's Purple Heart. Envelopes with the first hair of children now themselves grown gray or bald. But he'd never noticed Grandma's diary, or even known she'd kept one.

It was on the bottom, under the Normal School diploma she'd gotten at sixteen that was her ticket to a forty-dollar-a-month job teaching a dozen kids in the log school a mile down the road from where she was born. Adrian dusted the glass over the diploma and carefully replaced the relics he'd dug out. Gripping the tattered diary, he descended the steep attic steps.

He returned the flashlight to its drawer and tiptoed back to the bedroom. She was asleep, so he settled back into the creaking rocking chair to examine the book by dim lamplight. Only after some moments did he realize that her breathing had ceased.

He laid the diary on the nightstand and picked up her limp hand. No pulse. She was gone. On her mouth the hint of smile remained. In spite of the deep furrows, her face seemed somehow delicate, almost soft. Except for those lips, cracked and parched, eroded by eighty-eight years of sun and wind and dust.

Adrian turned down the quilt, folded his grandmother's wiry arms across her lean stomach, and pulled the cover up to her chin. He gazed a long moment at her peaceful face, kissed her cheek, and settled back in the rocking chair.

The first diary entry was 1913. Grandma was twenty, a veteran of four years of teaching, and Grandpa had just proposed marriage. Adrian read a couple of pages of oblique references to their courtship, then leafed to 1919, the year they'd moved to the Panhandle with four kids, a hundred quart jars of fruit and vegetables, a dozen hens and everything else they owned, rolled across 200 miles of Oklahoma prairie to a homestead west of the Cherokee Outlet. It was a haven of horse thieves and outlaws known as "Robbers' Roost," and "No Man's Land."

Entries here were short and occasional. There was too much work, too little time to write, but what there was conveyed happiness and strength. The birth of another child. Good wheat crops. Occasional social events, like the circus that got off the train in Boise City in 1924. Good prices in the mid-twenties, the new house in 1927. Life was stark, but for the hardy, life was good.

He thumbed on to 1929, December 1. "Andrew took a load of wheat to town today and came back with bad news. The market has crashed, and wheat is down to 40 cents. It costs more than that to grow it and send it on the train. I don't know how we'll make our land payment. At least we have food."

Adrian paged on, stopping at random. "July 2, 1934. A government man came today and wants to shoot the livestock. Says this will raise prices. Andrew blew up, threw the man out of the house. Said if there's any shooting on our place it won't be the cows. Already lost nearly half in a dust storm a month ago. Suffocated or got pneumonia, I don't know. The rest eat mostly tumbleweeds and are mighty poor. But at least we get a little milk and it keeps us alive."

"December 14, 1935. Andrew is practically crazy with rage. Went to the bank to borrow money to pay land taxes. Banker demanded 25 percent interest, but there was nothing else we could do. Deeper in debt every day. Got a letter from Mother last week. She says we should come home, it's not so bad there. We could stay awhile in the old log cabin Dad built on the Cimarron bluff when I was a child. We may have to if there's no rain next spring and no crops again. This is the fifth year. But Andrew says no, we'll see it through somehow. I just don't know."

"May, 30, 1936. The Luttrels left yesterday. Didn't even have a sale, since nobody's able to buy. Just loaded what would fit on the truck and headed west and left the rest behind. That makes six this spring that have gone. Just a handful still hanging on. The nearest neighbor now is the Parkers, three miles south."

"April 14, 1935." The page was worn and ragged. Dirt and blotches, perhaps tears, had smeared the dull pencil record. "The black blizzard began again last night. There was a little rain Sat., and Andrew and the boys had begun to plow the north field. This morning there was so much dirt against the front door it took two to push it open. Andrew went to the barn to check the three cows we have left, and Arnold went to the field to bring the tractor up. Andrew told him not to go, but he insisted. Said he'd follow the fence down and not get lost. He left with a wet rag over his face. He wasn't back in two hours so Andrew went to look for him. But now the dust is so bad I can't even see the barn. Andrew's been gone for over an hour too and I'm scared sick. I don't even know why I'm writing this, maybe to keep from screaming or crying. I have the younger children scooping dirt out of the house and covering the windows with blankets, mostly just to keep them busy. If the men aren't back in ten minutes, I'm going as far as the barn myself, but I dare not go farther. The other four will need me."

And then, "Later. The worst and the saddest of days. Andrew came back, but Arnold did not."

Outside, the wind howled like a ferocious beast. Windows rattled and rafters creaked. Little pyramids of snow had grown at the ends of the window sill. Grandma's face was white like snow. Adrian turned out the lamp and closed his eyes.

When he awoke, dawn had come. The wind's fury was spent and the snow had ceased. The eastern sky was red, tinting Grandma's watery pictures an eerie shade of blood. The diary had slipped from Adrian's fingers and lay open on the floor. He wanted to sleep again, even to dream of wind and dust, to forget that it was Christmas and Grandma was dead. But that wasn't her way. There were things that must be done.

A CHANGE OF WORLDS

"The dead are not powerless" —*Chief Seattle*

Oklahoma Territory, April 18, 1892

Reuben Westerfield pushed aside his blanket and raised to an elbow, his body stiff from sleeping on cold ground, and from the forty miles he'd walked since Enid. He opened his canteen and drank. Fires flickered or blazed as far as he could see down the Cimarron. Figures crouched or moved amongst the shadows, silhouetted against the smoky orange glow. Reuben stretched his back and got to his knees. Peering at the still shapes in the starlight around him, he strapped the canteen to his belt, then rolled his food box, tool pouch, and the Colt revolver into the blanket. He tucked in the ends and cinched the bundle with a scrap of rope.

In the makeshift tent behind him, a baby cried. Reuben stood and picked up his roll. The blanket door of the lean-to flapped aside and a man came out. "Baby got a fever," the man said. "You folks hasn't got medicine, does you?"

"Sorry," Reuben said. "It's just me and I'm traveling light."

"Thankee sir," the man said. He picked up a stick and stirred the coals of a smoldering fire, reddening his patched overalls and charcoal face. "She been sick since Fort Smith, but now she worse," he said. He shook his head and raised his eyes to the west. "I sho do hope to get a piece of that lan'. Maybe she be aright when we there."

"Yeah," Reuben said. "Don't we all. I hope she'll be O.K."

"Hey, knock off the chatter, darkie," snarled a voice from a tamarack clump to Reuben's south. "I can't believe they're lettin' you niggers run anyhow. There's more hard-workin white men than there is land, folks that can make something out of this."

"The Good Book say the meek shall inherit the earth," the black man answered. He crawled back into his tent. The baby was quiet now.

The other man crouched in the bushes and touched an ember to a cigarette, illuminating a lean and whiskered face. "Damn Indians don't need this land," he said. "These Cheyennes and Arapahos ain't even from here, I heard. This is just where they stuck 'em. Reservation, they call it. Well I got reservations myself." His laugh turned to a hacking cough and he spat.

"Been over, have you?" Reuben said in a low voice. He squinted for a better look at the man.

"Hell yes, ain't you?" The man sounded surprised. "They got more than they can use anyhow, the claim agent said so. Surplus land. What the hell, Indians don't know the value of land. What this territory needs is white farmers and cattlemen. Why let four million acres of good farmland go to waste?"

"Makes sense," Reuben said. He turned his back and waited for the other man to disappear. A sudden gust whipped a flurry of sparks from the Negro's fire.

When Reuben glanced back, the other man was not in sight. He crept to the tamaracks at the water's edge. He found a hole under a tangle of roots and shoved the bundle in. He ventured into the river, his eye on the western bluff. He waded until the water reached his armpits. Campfires and starlight reflected from the smooth surface. He leaned into the current, his arms above his head.

The Cimarron was wide and no doubt usually shallow, but in April it was high. The water was cold, and he began to swim, half floating, the gentle current carrying him along. Finding the bottom, he waded toward shore. He came out dripping on a sandbar and plunged quickly into a dome of willows.

He crouched shivering in a little clearing, the bluff looming high in the western sky. "Upland might be dry," he muttered to himself, "but it's bound to grow wheat." He was glad he had seed back in Kansas.

Reuben picked out the North star. He stumbled onto a trail of sorts, and followed it south. Deer? No, the brush was cleared too high. It had to be Indians. He'd heard some were still around. Unhappy with their allotments, apparently. But they got first choice, the papers said, and they were paid for the rest. He hoped it was true.

Reuben recalled the other run in '89, to the "Unassigned Lands." God, what a place that was. He'd staked a good claim, maybe fifty miles downstream from here. He'd had Charley then, and Charley was fast, Texas racehorse stock. He chuckled, picturing the others eating Charley's dust. He'd slept that night under these same stars, his future secure. He couldn't wait to bring Ruth to those rolling hills, the bottomland, the spring, the big native grass. But at sunrise he woke in the shadow of a dirty ragged man, a double-barreled shotgun poked in his face. He could still smell the cold oily steel. It had been a long ride back to Kansas. He'd gambled everything, but lost his claim. He should have brought a gun.

The trail veered away from the river and ran closer to the bluff. It was dark in the brush, and a branch lashed his face. He raised his arm as a shield and plunged on. It was a matter of hours now, after three long years. Ruth would be happy again if they could just settle down. Maybe have some kids. She'd never complained, and she didn't blame him. But she was tired of moving, always packing or unpacking the trunk, him blacksmithing in Hutchinson, laying rails in Wichita, bucking bundles clear to Fort Dodge, moving and waiting, like thousands of others, waiting for another run.

All summer he'd harvested wheat, a record crop for other men. But bust his gut as he would, they'd saved just twenty dollars. At least he'd gleaned some seed wheat, enough for ten acres. But then he'd lost Charley, which narrowed his options. Funny how a step in a gopher hole could change a man's fate. He was on foot this time, but he did have the Colt.

The path petered out in towering cottonwoods, but Reuben kept his southerly course. Then suddenly the flat broke off and he plunged down a bank to a stream. He knelt and dipped his hand to drink. The water tasted salty.

Instead of crossing the creek, he turned up the north bank and followed it west. The bed rose steadily into a canyon of blackjacks and then ash, and in ten minutes he emerged from the trees into open prairie, a world of stars and grass. Reuben strode across the plain, his legs switching through lush buffalo grass and bluestem. He mounted a ridge, then descended to another stream, much smaller, likely a tributary of the salty creek. He tasted again, and the water was sweet and cold. The spring had to be near. He followed this stream past wild plums, their hominy-smelling blossoms glowing white against the dark plain. A shallow valley sloped toward him.

Reuben found the spring in a jumble of rocks and dropped to his knees. "Spring Creek," he said out loud, and he rolled back his head and laughed to the stars. "It might not be original, but Spring Creek it is." He thrust his hands into the damp soil and squeezed a ball of sticky mud between his fingers. "God, rich!" he said. "Ruth, my dear, this is the place." He washed his hands and face, cupped his hands and took a long drink from the spring. He emptied his canteen and refilled it. He stood and strode back toward the bluff, his steps solid on the mellow soil, the sod he would break to grow wheat.

The prairie sloped gently back toward the bluff, and soon the now dim string of fires came back into view, less than half a mile away. Coming to the edge, he held to a sumac branch and peered over. "Too steep for a wagon," he said with satisfaction, "or even a horse." To get here by horse the route he had come would take time, maybe twenty minutes. But a man on foot could cross the river where it was deep and come straight up this bluff, and faster. He smiled. He would be here first.

Now to find the marker. He followed the bluff north until he found the little pile of stones, the corner of the quarter. He crouched by the pile and fingered the stones. They were cold and hard. There weren't enough here for a fireplace, but maybe a hearth. Reuben shivered in his still-damp clothes. He stood and hurried back the way he had come.

April 19, 1892. Eleven o'clock.

As far as Reuben could see, north or south, there were people, thirty thousand, somebody said. A permanent cloud of dust hung in the humid spring air. Some had been here for days, and they guarded their positions at the water's edge. Between him and the river, two men with horses trimmed a hoof with a knife. In the tamaracks beside him, the lean man was oiling a big revolver. A nasty scar blazed across the man's cheek, raw beneath the dust. The black family to his rear were rolling up their makeshift tent.

Reuben knew that others besides himself and the scarred man had crossed the river and picked a place. Maybe somebody else had picked his. All he had to do now was get there first. There weren't many like him, on foot. All along the line, horses stamped impatiently in the dust or strained against the lines of buckboards and wagons. Just to his north was a rickety wagon with a woman and five kids, not even a man. Reuben was glad he'd left Ruth in Kansas. She'd be here soon enough.

Scarface came out of the tamaracks and stooped to unhobble his big dark roan. He turned the horse toward the river and glanced contemptuously at Reuben. "Where's your horse?" he sneered. "Gonna do her on foot?"

"That's right," Reuben answered. He stared straight into the scornful eyes, wild outlaw eyes that reminded him of the claim-jumper. There were plenty of others like him too. Gamblers and bootleggers had worked the crowd for days, and their pockets were full.

The black man and his boy finished with their scraps of canvas. The woman was washing a cooking pot, the baby fretting listlessly at her breast. Another child drew in the dust with a stick. The family stood out like the black eye of a daisy in a sea of dusty white. "How's the baby?" Reuben asked.

"She not cryin'," the woman replied, "but maybe she cain't no more. We got to get her to a place."

"Just be sure it's nowhere near mine," growled Scarface. He advanced as he talked, and Reuben saw that he dragged a foot, like a coyote escaped from a trap. "You darkie sharecroppers think you can run a farm? I doubt it. I'll give you a year and then I'll buy you out. All you dirt scratchers think you're gonna be rich, don't you? Maybe you can grow cotton, but you don't know the first thing about hangin' on. Now me, I'm too smart to even try. Pure speculation, that's my line. If the price is high I sell, an if it's low I buy. And free Indian land is about as low as it gets." He laughed and bit off a plug of tobacco.

Reuben turned his back and glanced down the west-facing line. How many here would do anything for a quarter-section of land? And it wasn't just the crooks and claim-jumpers either. It was men like himself, men who knew the Indian land was nearly gone, that it was now or never.

It was almost noon. The human snake writhed and strained against the river's edge. The dust cloud hung low over the line, drifting aimlessly north toward Kansas, the place from which lots of others besides Reuben had come, at least most recently. The two men in front tightened their saddle straps. The woman on his right scolded the kids in the wagon to keep them still while she bound a splint to a cracked wagon spoke.

"Need help with that?" Reuben called.

"I'll manage," she said. "Been doing for myself for quite some time now. Thanks anyway." Her face burned red from sun and exertion.

Nervous shouts rang along the river's edge. There was an energy here that Reuben knew, this lust for land. And he knew the poverty, the secret shame, the failures and regrets. But there was fierceness too, a drive that was the offspring of powerlessness. At noon it would all explode. He'd seen it before, in '89—the violence, the energy, the thrust. By nightfall it would all be over. This community would still exist, but transformed, and new under the sun. Tent towns up and down the river, wagons crouched and rude shelters built throughout the valleys and the hills. It would no longer be surplus land.

Reuben's watch said 11:55. He squinted south into the sun, already hot. His eye traced the tree-lined bluff once more, searched the valleys to the south and measured the cottonwoods at the mouth of the salty creek. The bottom land looked good, but it was too far away. As always his eye came to rest where the red cliff rose, almost perpendicular, it seemed from here. In less than an hour he would drive his stake. By nightfall his blanket would be stretched over dead branches to form a crude shelter, not to protect him from the night, but so he could fall asleep thinking, "my land."

He would build a dugout, then a sod room, and some day a log or framed house. He wouldn't need a well, at least not now; the spring flowed enough for a garden and trees. Maybe later he'd dig a well and get cattle. On this land they would work and love and have children, and someday, when his children had children, he would lie below the sod.

It was two minutes 'til noon. The milling and maneuvering was intense, thousands elbowing for position, conversations all but ceased. Horses stamped, and people waited in the heat and the dust.

A man in a string tie stood up on a wagon a hundred yards down the river and waved his arms for quiet. He introduced himself as Tom Tayler, from Hennessey, the new town fifteen miles back east. He welcomed folks to the territory and explained again the process of staking a claim, which everybody here knew by heart. Somebody handed him a gun.

Reuben checked the rope on his bundle again. He had biscuits and dried meat for a few days, water, his papers, his stake, a few tools, and the Colt. It had cost him plenty. Everybody wanted one, it seemed. He cinched the bundle and strapped it to his back. He was ready. "Another minute," said a man in front. Reuben gazed straight ahead, concentration centered in his ears and his legs, listening for the shot, ready to run.

The revolver exploded and they were off. Reuben plunged through the tamaracks and into the river, waded until the familiar cold water touched his armpits, then swam, fast this time. His bundle was heavy on his back, but as before, the current tugged him toward his goal. When his feet touched bottom, he strained and sloshed to shore and ran, over the sand, through the willows, up the grassy slope to the bluff.

It was even steeper than he thought, and loose. He clawed and slipped, tried another spot, and another. Finally he grasped clumps of grass and pulled himself up to the hanging roots of a blackjack oak. Hand over hand he scrambled and pulled until he reached the top. He swung his legs over the edge, stood and sprinted to the pile of stones.

He dropped panting to the earth, stripped off his bedroll, untied the rope. He pulled out his stake and stabbed the sharpened point into earth. He seized a large stone from the pile to drive the stake in. His arms were raised to strike when he saw the skull, peering from the pile where he'd taken the stone. The surface was dull, the forehead round, the teeth grinning, one missing in front. From the deep hollow sockets, dark eyes burned into his for an instant and then were gone.

He dropped the boulder. One by one he picked away the stones, until the skull was free. He touched its smoothness, then lifted it out. The wide round sockets were empty, unbroken circles, two floating questions over high cheekbones. His own mouth formed another O. "Who?" it asked, and "How?" "What now?" Reuben shook the image from his brain. He knelt by the pile and carefully balanced the skull atop the stones. He picked up the boulder and pounded in his stake.

For the second time in his twenty-six years, Reuben had land. The blue devils that for three years had pursued him would be laid to rest. He sprawled on his elbows in the grass, the revolver on his lap. He raised his canteen and took a long drink of Spring Creek water. Eyeing the stones again, he saw that some were charcoaled, as if by ancient fires.

Over the southern ridge a dark horse and rider appeared, streaking toward him through a whirlwind of dust, hooves pounding the mellow sod. Reuben remembered the scar-faced man he'd encountered on the other side, and his fingers found the revolver and gripped it tight. As the horse drew near, he recognized the roan stallion. The man rode hard, straight toward him, neither slackening nor veering when he saw Reuben by the pile of stones. When he reigned hard at last, a cloud of dust filled Reuben's eyes. Reuben's finger was on the trigger, the barrel of the revolver aimed at the rider's heart. "So feet are faster than you thought," Reuben said in a voice calm but lethal. "Spur that horse or you're a dead man." Without a word the man rode on.

When he was gone, Reuben stood to his feet and surveyed the land, the first good look by daylight. "My land," he called out, then louder, "My land!" He glanced back at the pile of blackened stones. His would not be the first fire they had seen. His eyes could not avoid the penetrating gaze of the skull, the searching sockets that magnetized his brain. "Our land?" he asked. The gentle breeze that wafted up from the river brought no answer but the distant din of horses and wagons and men.

THE TENTH PART OF LAW

The first tinge of pink lighted the eastern sky across Spring Creek. Frost was heavy on the bluestem and buffalo grass and on the brittle brown leaves of the oak where James Westerfield sat on a limb that arched across the water. His breathing was the only sound, each exhalation forming an ethereal cloud that quickly vanished. He tried to get comfortable, shifting his weight to the other thigh.

A twig snapped, and James glanced upstream. He squinted and searched the tangle of plum bushes and cottonwoods on the north bank as far as he could see, then back down the grassy south bank to his tree. Nothing. Eyes and ears straining to the west, he waited. How many falls had he done this? Thirty-eight minus ten? He was ten the first time his father had brought him. So that would have been seven years for the two of them together, then just him for over twenty years. He had farmed this quarter on Spring Creek for all those years, first alone, then with Sarah's help. He was a good farmer and a good hunter too; he knew, and he loved this land. Sarah loved it too, as much as he did, the wife he had married eight years ago when he had given up on marrying, thinking he would be husband all his life to just the land. It was all he knew, and before Sarah, all he needed.

He had run the farm alone since just after his eighteenth birthday, the winter his father was thrown from the horse he was breaking in the corral just beyond the cottonwoods. James was a senior then, and he hadn't gone back to school. There was too much lost, and too much to do, but also he felt no need for more school. He'd never wanted to do anything but farm, never wanted to live anywhere but beside Spring Creek on the farm his great-grandfather had homesteaded in the Run of 1892.

James remembered why he was here and scanned the banks again. The big buck would be coming soon. He'd watched it all fall, earlier grazing near the cattle, then locking horns with other bucks in pursuit of does. Now that season had passed, and like James, the buck was content to pass his days guided by the rhythm of the creek.

Much had changed in the generations since Reuben Westerfield had taken this quarter in '92. Most of the land had long grown alfalfa and wheat, though along the creek native prairie remained. Most of the trees were second growth, but the fruit trees and a few others his grandfather had planted. One ancient cottonwood remained in the grove his great-grandfather spared, instead hauling cottonwoods up the steep bluff from the Cimarron to build the log house that still stood beside the barn, now a tool shed. His grandfather had built the newer house, a strong frame structure with a hearth and chimney made of rocks from the creek where James now waited. His grandmother, his mother, and his wife had borne children here, and now his grandparents and his father lay in the little cemetery on the ridge.

Recalling family history set James' nerves on edge. Not because he wasn't proud of the traditions he had inherited and maintained, but because recently he had begun to fear that this way of living might end with him. His own son and daughter loved the place just as he did, but for the first time in almost a century of Westerfields, living somewhere else seemed all too real a possibility.

In the two decades James had farmed, the price of wheat had declined, while the cost of everything they had to buy had more than doubled. Three summers had been dry and crops short, yet wheat had dropped to $2.50 a bushel, not enough to make the mortgage payment. James had inherited the place free and clear, but most of the machinery was worn out, and to compete he'd had to modernize. That meant borrowing money, something Grandpa John had warned him never to do. Each year he'd slipped a little deeper into debt, until the day five years back when he was forced to mortgage his great-grandfather's claim to pay interest on his debts. Alone in the barn that night, James cried like a baby, something he hadn't done since his father's death. His eyes moistened now, remembering. He wiped his jacket sleeve across his eyes, and squinted east into the growing light.

Then he saw it, where it must have been all along. The deer was now so well defined against a rosy horizon he marveled he had not seen it before. It raised its antlers from the water and gazed up the stream toward his tree, sniffing the air for something vaguely unfamiliar.

It drank again, then turned with a jerk and strode up the sandy bank toward him. Silently James raised his rifle. He clicked the safety and brought the sight to his eye. The deer was by the big cottonwood now, not more than fifty yards away, still moving toward him. Another moment. He drew a deep breath, felt the trigger, breathed out. Crack! A shot from downstream rolled up the creek and echoed back. The deer dropped. Amazed, James lowered his rifle unfired, transfixed by the death thrashing of the buck. Then in the cottonwood he saw movement, a man climbing down.

The man dropped from the bottom limb, leaned his rifle against the trunk, and scrambled down the bank. He pulled a glinting knife from his belt, knelt and slit the deer's throat. The man was on his knees, his fingers on the big buck's nose as blood gushed from its throat and puddled on the wet sand.

James returned to himself and set the safety on the Winchester. Grasping the muzzle, he lowered the gun and leaned it against the tree. When he jumped, the other man glanced up, searching for the source of the crash. James picked up his rifle, slid down the sandy bank, and with rifle lowered, trotted toward the other man and the deer.

"What are you doing hunting on my place?" James called out as he approached. The man, still crouched by the deer, pivoted to face him, the bloody knife still gripped in his hand. James saw that the man was an Indian. His hair was long black braids, his eyes narrowed slits. The fingers of his left hand still rested on the nose of the buck.

"This is my deer," the Indian said calmly. "My people have always hunted here. And my children are hungry." With that he wiped the blood from his knife on the brown grass and slipped it back under his belt. He turned back to the animal, whose eyes now gazed lifelessly at the widening sky.

"But this is my land," Westerfield protested. "You can't hunt here without my permission, which I don't give." He felt the blood rising in his face. "This is private property," he continued. "It's been in my family for four generations, and nobody hunts here but Westerfields. Now take your rifle and get off my place."

James was galled to find anybody on his land, let alone shooting deer, and an Indian to boot. His surprise was all anger now, and he swallowed to control his trembling voice. "Now get off or I'll call the sheriff," he said as calmly as he could. The Indian made no move to rise. He turned back to face the deer as if alone and watched the trickle of blood still seeping from the buck's throat and mouth.

James heard a rustle on the south bank. It was his daughter, his oldest child. She had heard the shot and come to see. "Rosa," he hollered, "go tell your mother to call the sheriff. We've got a trespasser here who's shot a deer. Probably doesn't have a license either." The girl turned and ran.

James stepped forward and grasped the intruder's collar, jerking him up. The man stood, and James saw how tall he was. There was defiance, but also a flat immobility in the other's eyes, a fearlessness, or indifference. "Now get your gun and go," James repeated, their faces close together now. Still the man did not move. Enraged, James shoved the other man hard toward the creek. The man stumbled, caught his balance and turned. His fist shot out and caught Westerfield's jaw, lifting him off the earth. James tumbled back and sprawled full length on the ground, his rifle slipping from his hands. His head struck a rock, and his mouth flew open in surprise. The branches of the cottonwood streaked away to infinity and James' body went limp in the sand.

When he came to, the Indian knelt above him, holding James' hand with one of his, feeling the blood pulsing through his wrist with the other. A shiny braid hung above James' face. The other man was about his age, but his hair was black, not graying like his own. Their eyes met, and James saw in the dark eyes what looked like sorrow or pain.

The Indian rose and went to the stream and cupped his hands. He returned, knelt by James' side and held his hands to James' lips. Cold water trickled down his cheeks. The Indian reached one hand behind James' head and wiped his forehead with a wet bandana.

"I'm sorry," the man said. "Your head hit a rock. Are you O.K.?"

James wasn't sure. His hand came up and gingerly groped for a gash on the back of his throbbing head. His fingers found warm sticky blood. "Here, let me fix that," the Indian said. He dipped the bandana in the water again and wrung it out. He raised James to sitting and gently wiped the wound on his head. Then James saw the deer, and he remembered.

"Who are you?" he demanded. "You didn't have permission to hunt here."

"I'm Lance Whirlwind," the other replied softly. "My great-grandfather was Whirlwind, a Cheyenne chief. My grandfathers have always hunted on this creek, before the white man came with his fences and cattle."

"But this isn't your land anymore," James interrupted. "Your people were given allotments before the white people came."

"Allotments!" Whirlwind repeated with a jeer. "President Grant drove us from the mountains and the plains to this little corner of our land. They told us this reservation would be ours forever. When the white men killed all the buffalo, there were still deer and turkeys on this and other creeks, and we still hunted on our land to feed our children."

"But this isn't your land anymore," James repeated, his mind clearing and his anger rekindling. "My great-grandfather staked a claim on this quarter a hundred years ago. Your people were paid for this land!"

Now the kindness James thought he'd seen in the other's eyes vanished. Whirlwind spat on the ground. "One dollar an acre," he said through his teeth. "But the land was not for sale. The chiefs turned it down. The agents had to cheat and threaten old women and children to find enough people to sign. They didn't buy this land. They stole it." His voice was low and deliberate, but in the tone of a moderated curse.

James was quiet now, as Whirlwind tied the bandana around his head, covering the gash. "When the white men in Washington forced us to this reservation in 1875, there were over 6,000 of us Cheyennes and Arapahos. In two years the buffalo were gone, and my people began to starve. In ten years half of us were dead. So the government gave us beef, but always skinny cows, not like the buffalo. And every time they wanted to take more of our freedom away, they cut the rations again. They forced us to send our children to their schools, they took away our religion, they wanted us to be farmers like them, to build fences around the land, to sell our Mother Earth. If we gathered in our camps for ceremonies, they drove us apart and put our chiefs in jail. If we didn't go along with what they said, they cut the rations again and we watched our children and grandmothers starve."

"But this was surplus land," James insisted. "The government let you pick your allotments before white people came in. Your people got the best land, the valleys of the Washita and the Canadian, the best soil and the best timber in the country. Anyway," he said, matching the other man's defiant tone, "Possession is nine-tenths of the law."

"Yes," Whirlwind went on, as if reciting an ancient story by heart. "The best land. But my grandfather didn't want to own

160 acres like your grandfather. He wanted to live in the old way with his tribe in the camp. Just twenty miles west of here at Canton, that's where my people lived. I've heard my grandfathers tell of the beautiful valley they finally took and agreed with the white men to stay there. There was much timber on that place then, and many deer. But the white men came down from the hills with their wagons and cut the timber and hauled it away to build houses and barns and to sell for more silver dollars. Then the deer disappeared too."

James struggled to get his feet under him and stood up. He swayed and staggered, but caught himself and leaned against the tree. He felt faint and strange. He touched the wound on his head again. He was aware of the pounding of his heart. He wanted to get this man off his place, deer and all if necessary, but he had no clear idea how to do that now. The Indian still knelt by the buck. He was drawing something in the wet sand with his finger.

"Later the government took even the land of my grandfathers' camp," he said. "They built a dam on the Canadian to make a lake for motor boats and tourists. My grandfather's lodge is under Canton Lake now. Maybe you've fished over my grandmother's grave," he said with a bitter laugh. He rose and faced James again, and his quiet voice rolled on.

"When the government men offered money they told the chiefs, 'You will be the wealthiest people on Earth.' But the chiefs did not want to sell the land. Old Crow pointed to the ground. 'Here is my wealth,' he said. 'Here is all the wealth I want.' But they took the land anyway. They took most of our land then, and what little was left is lost now. So when our children are hungry, we hunt for food to feed them."

Whirlwind's soft voice stopped and it was apparent he had finished. James turned again to the deer, considering. The sun had risen, brilliant and clear. A flicker called from a dead limb of the cottonwood.

A horn honked on the ridge, and James glanced up to see the sheriff's car bumping slowly down the lane. He turned to the Indian again, expecting fear or flight. Instead, the other stood with arms folded, his eyes narrowed and penetrating. Whirlwind stood still and waited. The car disappeared for a time, then reemerged past the barn, moving steadily toward the creek. The car nosed up to the south bank and stopped and the sheriff got out.

"Howdy, James," the sheriff called across Spring Creek. "Got a little trouble here?" Then the sheriff saw Whirlwind's passive waiting face. "Another Indian poacher?" he said with a nod. "We've got room for him in the county jail in Watonga." The sheriff felt his revolver, and began looking for a place to descend the steep bank.

"It's O.K., Clarence," James called back suddenly, and the utterance surprised him as much as it did the sheriff. "It's just a misunderstanding," he added, embarrassed now. "There won't be any need to take him in. I'm sorry I bothered you."

The sheriff looked doubtful. "Are you sure?" he called back, pausing on the edge of the caving bank. "You can't be too careful."

"It's O.K.," James repeated. "Thanks for coming out." The sheriff hesitated another moment, then got back into his car and backed away from the edge.

When he was gone, James turned to Whirlwind. "This deer should be gutted," he said. "Is your knife sharp?"

BOOTLEGGER'S REVENGE

The Ford wasn't new, but to Arlo Stinson it was. And man, would that V-8 cruise. Everybody thought he was crazy in the middle of a Depression to spend good money on a three-year-old car when the Model A still ran and most of the neighbors had trouble putting food on the table. But harvest was over and Arlo had a little money in his pocket. "You only live once," he said with that laugh that reminded his friends he wasn't a guy to worry himself about next year.

The windows were open and Blanche's red hair whipped like a fox tail in the wind. Maggie bounced on Blanche's knee and clapped to Bob Wills' new song on the radio, "I'm Sitting on Top of the World." In the rearview mirror a cloud of red dust rose, swirled and hung on the calm air for a quarter mile back. When Arlo brought his eyes back to the road, he saw through a tangle of hackberry trees a similar trail of dust, perpendicular to his and heading his way, the glint of steel and glass in the corner of his eye. Arlo stomped the brake, but already the Chevrolet was in the intersection, hurtling toward them. There was Billy Wainwright's face—his mouth gaping in surprise—as the Chevrolet slammed into Arlo's '32 and they were rolling and spinning and Arlo was flying toward the sunflowers in the ditch and then the car was coming too and when it stopped the front fender landed with a thud on his chest, the still-spinning wheel kicking dust in his face.

Arlo blinked away the dust, and the racing wheel slowed until he registered individual spokes, and finally the whirling stopped and the only sound was something dripping on his leg. Then from somewhere in the gathering dusk a sorrowful moan.

He rolled his head one way and then the other, but couldn't locate the sound. It was Blanche.

The whimper came closer, and finally he saw her, crawling toward him, her face streaked with blood. "Maggie," the voice wailed, "Where is Maggie? I can't find my baby! Where is Maggie?" Blanche disappeared from Arlo's vision and the cries moved to the other side of the car, and suddenly the wail became a hysterical shriek. "Maggie! Maggie! Oh my God, Oh my Maggie!" And then uncontrolled sobs and screams.

Arlo tried to call out to Blanche, but he couldn't catch his breath. He squirmed until he could get both hands under the fender and strained with all his might, but the weight on his chest refused to budge. Something strange filled his throat and he choked and gasped for air. Blanche's cries came closer again, now almost coherent. "Maggie's gone, Oh my Maggie," she wailed. "Our baby is dead." She reappeared on Arlo's side of the Ford, still crawling, one arm cradling the limp form in the long flowered dress. She laid the terrible burden in the dust and then she was on her knees at his side, straining to lift the car. He added the little strength of his outstretched arms, and for a moment it seemed the pressure lessened on his chest, but then it slipped back, more oppressive than before.

Blanche cradled Arlo's head in her arms and buried her face in his neck. The long tresses draped his face with the fragrance of lilac and dust, and tears dampened his neck. He choked and coughed and tasted blood. He turned his head and it seeped from the corner of his mouth. Then, mingling with the dust and the perfume of Blanche's hair and the dripping gasoline, Arlo became aware of another scent, an odor familiar and sharp. And then he knew it, and squinting toward the overturned Chevrolet he saw mixed with the shattered windshield glass a broken jug. What he smelled was an acrid spray of moonshine liquor in the sand. He didn't know where Billy Wainwright lay, or whether he was alive or dead, but he knew where Billy had been.

And then Arlo was in that other summer night, the kind of night when the sweet aroma of alfalfa and dew intoxicated the mind, when the silence amongst the cottonwoods that lined Sandy Creek was broken only by the occasional hoots of owls. The sky was a canopy of stars so bright that Arlo and Alfred easily followed the well-worn path from the county road the quarter mile up the creek bank to Hally Deeter's still. It was well after midnight, and the quiet reassured them that both Deeter and his customers had called it a night. A glint of tin marked the place in the creek bank where Hally hid his mash and the apparatus that turned the grain he grew into a product far more valuable than what the elevator bought. Hally was smart enough not to leave the filled fruit jars here by the creek, of course. Those Arlo and Alfred knew were locked away in the cellar behind his barn.

The pair crept quietly along the trail, speaking not a word, watching for fallen twigs that might snap, Alfred carrying a small package with great care. Where the trail ended they pulled back branches that covered the tin, and opened the tarpaulin that served as a door. Arlo struck a wooden match on his dungarees and the pair stooped and crept inside. The flame reflected from the shiny copper of the boiler and the coil of tubing that led to a small bench lined with empty jars. The cave reeked of wood smoke, sour mash, and alcohol.

Alfred nestled the long smooth stick under the cooker and raked walls of sand around the edges to contain the blast. His uncle worked at the gypsum plant in the Glass Mountains, and he had slipped the dynamite out in his pants leg. "I wish he'd brought a longer fuse," Alfred whispered. "I don't know how long it takes three feet to burn. I hope long enough for us to get out of here and behind the trees." He attached the fuse, strung it toward the door, and flashed a big smile at Arlo. "You want to do the honors?" he asked.

Arlo pulled another match from his pocket and struck it on his pants. "Well, Mr. Deeter," he said, "say goodbye to your poison mill." Arlo touched the match to the fuse. Sparks and a low hiss said the fuse had caught. Arlo and Alfred stumbled out of the cave and ran, now thrashing headlong fifty feet down the trail to a fallen cottonwood. Over the trunk they sailed and sprawled in the sand. They peeked over the log just as the muffled blast blew the top off the hideout. The trees went bright and Hally Deeter's crumpled kettle hurtled skyward, crashing through branches, knocking off leaves and twigs, tumbling end over end to above the tallest tree, halting for what seemed an endless second, then crashing back through the branches to splash with a hiss in Sandy Creek.

In seconds it was over. Now the night was completely still, even the owls gone mute. Arlo punched Alfred and they issued a muffled laugh, and then they were on their feet and running again. No doubt Deeter heard the explosion, and by now he was out of bed and had his shotgun in his hands and would be coming out the door any second, and they didn't want to be anywhere around. The question was whether Arlo's father had been wakened by the blast. That was half a mile down the creek, but it was summer and the windows were open, so it was anybody's guess. If his father was awake, Arlo hoped he wouldn't check his bed, where he was supposed to be sound asleep.

Arlo opened his eyes. The stench of gasoline overpowered the aroma of moonshine. Arlo's pants were drenched now, but that didn't seem a reason for concern. In fact, the whole situation seemed less alarming than it had. He thought of his daughter, the lovely creature who had come into their home less than a year after he and Blanche had married. He felt sadness that she was gone, but it was difficult to focus on her face, and then the face blurred and it was Blanche above him again, the drying blood now smeared aside by her sleeve to clarify in the growing darkness the gashes torn by windshield glass, her lovely red hair matted with blood and dust, rivulets of tears washing down her cheeks, she still wailing and crawling and heaving against the immovable fender, still calling Maggie's name.

The sky was growing darker now, but myriad stars were
blinking on. Arlo rolled his head toward the Big Dipper,
followed the rim of the bowl up and focused on Polaris, the
north star, the heavenly body that had guided his feet many a
dark night. It seemed more distant than ever, and yet it was a
comfort that held his eyes and helped calm the commotion that
he now only wanted to go away. He tried to think of other
things besides the pain in his chest, the wild cries of the woman
who wept and screamed and labored at his side, the little girl
who lay a crumpled ruin in the dust.

He remembered nights tromping across open fields,
following the stars to Alfred's house. He recalled the swing
behind his parents' house, holding Blanche's cheeks in his
hands, kissing her upturned face under stars so bright they
reflected in her sky-blue eyes. He summoned images of his
father in the good days, how almost every skill Arlo possessed
his father had handed down. They had been so close when he
was a boy, working together in the fields, hunting coons along
the creek, good days and nights before the hard times, before
they lost the livestock and half their land, before the blue devils
that moonshine quelled.

He thought again of the still, and the night he and Alfred
blew it to the stars, not imagining that in a month it would be
running again, Deeter sitting late into the night with the
shotgun on his knees. He pictured the nights before and again
after when his father came stumbling home from Deeter's
place, the jug sometimes half full, other times not; the cruelty,
his mother's tears and prayers; the plan he made with Alfred to
end the pain, and how foolish they had been to think that a
stick of dynamite could end the needs of desperate men.

Arlo felt a gurgling chuckle rise in his throat at the
absurdity of their boyish scheme, the notion that a flash in the
night could change the course of history, could alter the nature
of men that drives them to defy a law that tells them what they
can't do, could stop the flow of the elixir that dulls the pain of

lost farms and broken dreams, and fills the pockets of some men by emptying the pockets of others.

But all that was blurry now, of little consequence. The sky was completely dark but for the stars, and even Blanche's face had lost its glow. Now she mumbled something about going for help and then she kissed him, her face wet with tears, and she was off, crawling and standing and stumbling down the dusty road toward a glowing farmhouse window a mile away. The only sound now was the steady drip-drip-drip of gasoline on his leg and his gurgling breath, which seemed hardly necessary anymore, for where would it get him anyway?

It occurred to Arlo that he should stand up and do something about the wreckage that surrounded him. He gathered his strength for one more try, but he could barely lift his arms. A tiredness he had never known was washing over him. He wanted to close his nostrils to the gasoline and the moonshine, and also to close his eyes, to blink away the shiny fender of the Ford that pinned him to the Earth. But when he did the other pictures returned; Maggie and Blanche, he and Alfred tiptoeing up the starlit trail to the still, the fire in his father's eyes when Arlo crawled back through the window, the fierceness with which he wielded the belt, a cruelty that clouded the good days and the nights when the whole world was his father and him, under the heavens.

So much pain, but apparently that was what life was about. So Arlo didn't close his eyes. He concentrated on the constellations, which required only a slight twist of his neck and no thinking at all. It was better, he decided, not to close the nostrils, not to close the eyes, to go on breathing as long as that were possible, to keep his eyes focused on the North star, around which the universe swirled.

THE PRICE OF LAND

Elmer Weber opened his eyes to a world of white. He saw a woman's face, and a shiny steel pole with a bottle and a rubber hose. All else was white: the ceiling, the walls, everything about the woman except her face. He noticed something on his forehead, something white, and a tightness above his eyes. The other sensation was a strangeness in his right arm, not pain exactly, but a certain numbness, something too vague to comprehend. Where was he now, and where had he been?

A smile formed on the face above his, and the lips moved, but Elmer could not comprehend the sounds, muffled as they were by the fading ring of a far-off bell. His eyes searched the room. Nothing was familiar.

The face went away, then returned, and fingers touched his face. The lips moved again, then in little jerks his body rose so that now a window appeared. Squinting into the light he made out a long row of low drab structures, something familiar, something he'd somewhere seen before. The hand brought a cup to his mouth. Something cool and wet touched his lips and he swallowed.

From the bottle above his head, liquid dripped into the hose. His eyes followed the hose to his left arm where it disappeared under more white. He looked at his other arm, but strangely it was hidden somewhere. Below his shoulder where the arm should have been there was instead a wrap of white cloth. He thought that strange, but not a reason for concern. He closed his eyes again and drifted off to sleep.

How much time had passed when he opened them again he did not know, but now the room was dark. The ringing gong was less intense, and it seemed now that he heard other sounds, small scurrying and murmuring sounds, possibly a voice somewhere. Through the window a dim light glowed. He tried to lift his head, but found it too heavy. His eyes shifted about the room, eventually coming to rest again on the place beside him where his arm should have been. He stared for a long while at the empty place. Little by little it came to him that his right arm was simply gone.

He lay contemplating this strange discovery until light outside the window began to grow. He thought once to explore this void with his left hand, but he discovered that it could not be moved. The wrap of white held it fast.

A door opened and another face appeared, another young woman. She came to Elmer's side, and it occurred to him to ask about the void at his side. He tried to form the word, but nothing came. What was the word? "Arm," he finally managed to utter. "My arm?"

The lips moved again, and applying all his will he did comprehend a mumble that surfaced above the ringing hum. There were sounds he recognized—"tank," and "shell," and "lucky." His mind struggled with the words. Shell and lucky he couldn't place, but yes, "tank," that was familiar. He locked on that word, and a fuzzy image formed in his brain. Yes, of course, his tank. And now he was bouncing across an open field, winter turnip greens and snow, and shells—yes, shells, exploding in front, coming his way. He was in the turret, the machine gun rattling with rage. But how did he get from there to here . . . and what of the empty place where his arm should have been? An overwhelming weariness swept over him, and again he closed his eyes.

When Elmer resurfaced from this stupor there was another voice, this one familiar, and sobbing sounds. He opened his eyes to a face he knew, hovering above his, tear-streaked cheeks and sorrowful eyes. It was his mother. She buried her face in his neck and wept. Behind the graying hair stood his father, clean overalls, sadly smiling, reaching to grasp his hand. There were more words, some he comprehended: "love" and "home." These were good words, and he felt content. But then he remembered the dark discovery in the night.

"My arm?" he asked.

His mother's sobs intensified. His father put his arms around her and gently tugged her away. Then with both his hands he grasped Elmer's left hand. "It's OK," he said. "For you the war is over. You're coming home."

Weeks passed, and the ringing subsided. The room, the faces, even the words grew familiar. Then came the lovely day in June when Elmer Weber stepped off the train in Okeene. It was summer now, and the afternoon heat reflected from the wheat elevator that loomed above, the elevator that before the war he'd helped build at thirty cents an hour. There was a line of trucks, loaded with golden wheat. He squinted into the sun, and a voice called his name. Rushing toward him were his mother and father, and two young women that must be the kid sisters he hadn't seen for years.

Elmer reached for his duffel bag, but his father grabbed it and insisted on carrying it. He tugged the bag across the platform and down the steps and heaved it into the back of the car. It was the same Model A Ford that had brought Elmer here in January 1941—a lifetime ago. Everybody hugged Elmer awkwardly and welcomed him home, and he hugged them back, as well as a man with one arm can do. Then the family climbed in for the ride to the farm.

For Elmer it was a long ride. It was just five miles, but for him it was a journey to another country, familiar yet strange, or perhaps to another century, to an era long ago when he drove this same Ford each morning from the farm to the filling station where he worked in town, the era when on Saturday night he and Louise might go the movie and afterwards have ice cream at the soda fountain in the hotel.

Then came the afternoon in 1940. He was changing oil in Jack Steiger's Chevrolet. On the radio they were talking about the lottery the government had set up to choose men for the first round of the military draft. Somewhere somebody drew a number from a fishbowl, and it was Elmer's number. It was the first number called. He had won the lottery, but what exactly did that mean?

At first there was something akin to elation. If America had to fight the Germans, he would be among the first to defend his country. And there was excitement too. The farthest from home he'd ever been was the county seat, and now he would see the world!

The government said the draft was for just a year. Louise promised to wait, and the boss said he'd try to take him back when he came home. So it was off to Fort Sill for basic and then to an armored outfit at Fort Benning, Georgia. Hitler was advancing across Europe, but so far America was staying out of the war, and soon Elmer's year would be up. Then in December the Japanese bombed Pearl Harbor, America declared war, and instead of coming home after Christmas as he'd expected, Elmer's service was extended for the duration of the war.

There was more training, then off to the other side of the world, the bloody campaign across northern Africa, the invasion of Sicily, followed by the grueling push north through Italy. And still the war dragged on. His division advanced northward, fought and died in the drive eastward across France, routing Germans all the way to Belgium in the summer of 1944, to the turnip field where at last an enemy shell scored a direct hit on Elmer's tank. Again he was the lucky one. He was blown free of the wreckage and into a crater, and only he survived. One eardrum was shattered, his face and torso were full of shrapnel, and his right arm was so mutilated that the only thing to do was amputate.

It had been a long four years, more than a lifetime long. There was news from home, but he knew his parents well enough to know the details were tempered to save him as much worry as they could. Much of the news was bad. Things weren't good on the farm. His boss at the gas station couldn't wait forever, and had replaced him with an older man. And worst of all, they couldn't hide from him the fact that Louise had married another man—the banker's son, who'd gotten a deferment from the draft because he claimed an injured back. Now Elmer was coming home at last, what was left of him, but to what? What would he do? He tried to hide his sorrow and fear. There must be jobs Elmer could do on the farm, and at least nobody was shooting at him anymore.

They rolled past fields ripe with wheat, others just stubble now, others where combines and trucks rumbled along in clouds of reddish dust. At last they topped the rise, and a shabby little house in a grove of elms came into view. The house didn't belong to them, but for half his life before the draft, it had been home. Like this farm and several others, it belonged to Gordon Robinson, the banker in town. It was what the Webers were able to find after they'd lost the farm they owned. So his father had signed on as a sharecropper, but with an agreement that if they got the money together they could make cash payments and begin to buy the farm. Unfortunately that hadn't happened. So Elmer's parents were beyond middle age and still farming the quarter-section on shares. But at least it was home.

When his sister opened the front door the aroma of bread nearly swept Elmer off his feet. Not even the pizzerias of Italy could hold a match to his mother's homemade bread. A fat hen browned in the oven, and potatoes and noodles simmered on the stove. The family gathered around the checkered oilcloth, Elmer now at the end opposite his father. Eating awkwardly with his left hand, he wolfed down the first home-cooked meal he'd had in years. It seemed almost possible that normal life might return.

It wasn't until the next day, out of his mother's hearing at the barn, that Elmer's father shared the bad news. Banker Robinson couldn't wait on the Webers any longer. He had announced his plan to sell the farm once the summer's hay was in. Robert Weber had no idea where the family would go or how they would survive. The down payment was a thousand dollars, and the Webers had $32 in the bank.

It wasn't the first time. Elmer remembered the good years of his childhood on the quarter section by the river, and how that all ended the year he turned 13. Wheat prices were high during and after World War I, and his parents had almost paid off the farm. Like several of his neighbors, Robert Weber decided to modernize. His plow horses were worn out and he had to make a change. Wheat was bringing a dollar a bushel, so in 1928 he bought a new John Deere tractor. Neither he nor his neighbors could have known that the good times were about to end. In 1930 the price of wheat dropped like a rock, and the next year it plunged to twenty-seven cents a bushel. Weber couldn't make the payment on the tractor, let alone the farm. The still shiny green tractor was repossessed by the implement dealer, and in 1931 the bank foreclosed. To recover its money, the bank auctioned everything Robert and Mabel Weber owned.

Well, not quite everything. Elmer was the oldest of three kids, his youngest sister not yet in school. The auctioneer sold the plow, the disk, the harrow, the wheat drill, the binder, and all the other implements. Then he moved on to the household goods, anything that would bring a price. Most everything went for a fraction of its true value, partly because most neighbors had no money to bid, or if they did have a little squirreled away they were ashamed to profit from their neighbors' misfortune. The livestock came last. Somebody from Major County bought the pigs, and the chickens went for pennies each to the produce man. They were down to Rosy, the milk cow. That's when the banker's compassion, or, more likely shame, kicked in. "Let them keep the cow," he muttered to the auctioneer. "Those kids have to eat." He turned his back and strode toward his Lincoln, and the sale was over. Neighbors mumbled condolences, and the few who had bought gathered their shabby new possessions and quietly departed. The Webers had another month in the house and no place to go, but they did still have a cow. They moved in with Mabel's folks for the winter, and in March the old Harper place, which also had been foreclosed, came up for rent.

Elmer chuckled at the recollection. "Well, Dad," he said. "it could be worse. Once again, we have no place to live, but at least now we have three cows." Robert laughed too, but it was a hollow laugh, barely masking the bitterness he felt, a bitterness he didn't want to inflict on his son.

For his part, Elmer threw himself into the farm work as best he could. A man with one hand can milk cows—in twice the time it ought to take. It was difficult to manage a tractor, because shifting and turning required two hands. There was little around the house he could do to help, and his mother seemed uncomfortable with his efforts. The Army had promised to fit him with a prosthesis once his stump completely healed, and they also promised a disability check. But two months had passed and he hadn't heard a thing. So the long days of summer dragged on, and whatever joy homecoming had brought wore thin. With each passing day Elmer's struggle with the blue devils was harder to master, even to mask. How could a man with one arm buck bales? He couldn't even help his mother kill and butcher chickens. He inquired about jobs in town, but got only awkward replies that he interpreted as "We'd love to hire a war hero, but we just don't have anything you could do."

September 1st came around, the last month before they had to go, and still no plan. They'd found no other farms for rent, no prospects for other jobs. Then on Thursday afternoon a new Ford pulled up the drive. It was a man from the War Department, come to assess Elmer's disability and determine a settlement. It was hard for Elmer to admit that after all he'd been through he was just half a man, but that was how he felt. The government man agreed, and put him on the disability roll at $50 a month. He made an appointment for Elmer to be fitted with a hook.

After supper Elmer borrowed the Model A and drove into town. The bank was closed, so he went to the Robinsons' house. The banker greeted him at the door, but didn't invite him in.

"I'm here to buy my parents' farm," Elmer said.

"Well, that's nice," the banker said, "but do you have the money? All the paperwork is at the bank. Why don't you and your dad come in tomorrow and we'll talk." He twisted the doorknob to go back in.

"Wait," Elmer said, grabbing Robinson's flabby arm with his strong left hand. "I want to make a deal now. No, I don't have the money, but I will have. You want a down payment of $1,000. My right arm was worth $50 a month to this country. In two years that will bring $1200. I'll sign that over to you right now. You'll get your down payment by the month, and the extra $200 adds 10 percent a year. That should be good interest, even for a bank."

"You don't understand," the banker said with an indulgent smile. "We can't wait any longer to recover our investment in this land. I don't want to be callous, but your folks have had years to put the money together. I'm afraid this just won't work."

Elmer's grip on the other man's arm tightened, and he pulled the banker close to his shrapnel-pocked face. "Listen to me," he said. "This will work, because you're going to make it work. While I was sleeping in the mud and watching comrades die, your son was making good money in your bank—and taking the girl I'd planned to marry. Now I'm back, and I may be just half a man in your eyes, but I'm here to tell you that you will make this work. I didn't come home from four years of war to watch my folks thrown out of their house and farm—again. An arm for a farm, that's the deal. I'll be in your office tomorrow morning to sign the papers."

When Elmer released Robinsons' arm the banker recoiled against the still-closed door. He returned Elmer's gaze for a long moment, his eyes conveying sullen resolve, but colored by fear or shame. He turned and opened his door without a word, but Elmer had no doubt the deal was done.

WHITE DREAMS

Coal Washington's big hands gripped the shovel handle, veins bulging in the flickering light of dying embers. Here and there a tongue of flame still played amongst the smoking ruins of what had been his home. Coal's massive shoulders sagged forward, his body balanced on the tripod of shovel and sprawled-out legs. The laces of his sodden work boots hung loose, and around his feet lay a tangle of garden hose. His jeans and longjohn shirt were soaked with water and sweat and splotched with soot. His eyes smarted from the smoke, and his brown face was streaked with sweat and tears.

Embers cooled from white to orange to dull red, and still Coal stood transfixed and stared into the darkening void. The chill night air crept up his still-wet legs, and when he moved at last, it was a shiver that shook his frame. A tautness like death possessed his muscles and bones, the stiffness of utter fatigue. Rousing his sleeping body at last, Coal picked up the shovel and began to move. The crackling sound was his jeans, frozen stiff on the backs of his legs. His teeth chattered, and now he moved consciously, closer to the fading warmth. He turned his back to the hearth, finding feeble warmth against the cold and black that stretched from the depth of his soul to the distant stars of the January sky.

A light wind stirred, and in the faint undulations of embers, Coal perceived dimly the outline of the barn. He shuddered again, dropped the shovel, and moved stiffly toward it. Inside he breathed the sweet steamy aroma of alfalfa and horses' breath. A cow lowed softly, and something bumped against a stall. Coal dragged his exhausted body up the ladder into the hayloft. He crawled into a pile of loose straw and covered himself. He closed his smarting eyes, and immediately he slept.

It was a large barn in which Coal Washington lay, a fine new barn. He had built it that summer, carrying and cutting lumber and driving nails in the morning and evening hours before and after field work. During the day he had a carpenter from town, a white man, and a couple of black neighbor boys to help. The barn was tall, built on the same low rise as Coal's house. The shiny corrugated roof could be seen for miles. The barn was built in the old style, with stalls and granaries and a hayloft, not like the cheap steel buildings people were throwing up these days. All through that summer as he made the rounds through his fields, harvesting and plowing and haying, Coal's satisfied gaze had rested on the rising barn.

The barn had been the last component of a massive dream, a dream that had grown in Coal's head for twenty years, a dream born the night six-year-old Coal lay alone in a cold bed, sobbing in humiliation, the night the sheriff came to bring foreclosure papers on his father's forty-acre farm. It was a dream—and more than a dream, it was a plan—which he had known for two decades could not and would not fail. It was a vision that Coal had shared with no one, not his broken father or his sorrowing mother, not his coach who urged him to take a basketball scholarship to the state university, not even the wife he had married three years ago as part of the dream.

"It seem like a black man jus can't make it in dis' worl'," his father had lamented over and over, sitting by the wood stove in the kitchen of the house he had once owned and where he'd stayed on as a sharecropper on land now owned by a fat insurance man in town. "It seem like de white man just want to put all de colored folks in one bag," Coal's father said. "Dey jus' wan' us to be slaves, one way or t'other."

Coal's father was an old man, and seemed an older man, even then. He had left Mississippi as a teenager on a freight train headed for Chicago, working at odd jobs until he landed work as a porter on a Santa Fe passenger train. He rode that train for twenty-five years, until one night he met a pretty young woman on her way back to Oklahoma from visiting an uncle in Chicago. He got off the train with her in Enid. They were married a few days later, and Mr. Washington took his meager savings out of the bank and made a down payment on a sandy forty near his bride's father's farm.

A year later Coal was born, the only child his parents would ever have. World War II was raging in Europe, and wheat prices were good. In the early years it looked as if the Washingtons might make it. They got a new stove, painted the house, and fixed the roof. Coal's earliest memory was of riding around the countryside with his father, looking for a bargain on a second-hand tractor. But the odds were against them. Interest rates were high, especially for a black man with just forty acres and a tired-out mule, and Washington had to borrow, even for seed and the necessary machinery and for a little fertilizer for a worn-out farm that a decade earlier had been the rim of the Dust Bowl.

Year after year Washington slipped deeper into debt. Then when Coal was five his appendix ruptured, and the doctor bills pretty well finished them off. The banker was patient for two more years. Why shouldn't he be? He knew he would get the forty in the end, worthless though it was. So Washington was left at age fifty-one with no farm, unpaid doctor bills, and the prospect of sharecropping for a white man the rest of his life.

There was rarely any spending money for Coal, sometimes not even enough for new school clothes. His mother patched and mended and somehow kept the family warm and fed, and in fact they were not much different from most of the neighbors, at least the colored folks. But Coal's father had seen the world, and he wanted more. He had served white men in suits for twenty-five years, and he didn't want to do that any more. He had grown up on a sharecropper farm, but now he had owned a farm, shabby though it was, and he powerfully resented his slide back into servitude. Fuming by the stove through the long winter months, he grew bitter and argumentative. Sometimes when his anger boiled over he struck Coal and his mother.

So Coal huddled by the woodstove in the kitchen, feeding on the bitterness of a broken father, angry at poverty and hopelessness, internalizing despair. But from some unlikely seed the other dream grew in his brain, a vision that denied the poverty and humiliation that lurked in the dark corners of the austere house, a vision of wealth and power and self-respect, a vision in which he commanded people and money and land, like the insurance man who came each fall after harvest to collect his rent.

At the colored school he attended, Coal had no reason to feel inferior. He was bright enough, and by third grade he was the biggest boy in his class. His clothes were no better or worse than the average. He earned recognition for his ability in sports, especially basketball. Other boys began to crowd around him in the locker room, or to share treats with him. He noticed that he could generally get them to do what he wanted. By fifth grade the girls noticed him too, though he showed little interest in them. But the next year, the big change came. The two schools in the community were integrated.

The white school and the colored school had coexisted just four miles apart for as long as anybody could remember, having little to do with one another. Buses sometimes met on the narrow country roads, taking white children west or black children east in this community where black people mingled with down-on-their-luck white people who had come from just about everywhere to this worn-out Cimarron River land. Coal knew most of the white neighbors by sight, and once when he was small the Watson boys down the road had come over to play. But this was a poor country farmed by poor people, and those who could moved on. Both schools were half empty, so when the government ordered schools integrated, the white school board simply closed the colored school, and when fall came, opened the doors of the white school wide, smiling with self-congratulation that the schoolhouse was full in a community where everybody was equal. Well, almost.

So Coal's mother laid out his best jeans and shirt and packed his lunch box with a ham and egg sandwich, and off he went to his new school. And that's where his own trouble began. Coal was still the biggest boy in sixth grade, but a couple of white boys thought he shouldn't be, and took it upon themselves to take him down to size. So Coal, who had been peaceable before, had to fight. The first day, he came home with a rip in his best shirt and a bloody nose. His mother cried softly as she mended the shirt, but his father raged at "whitey," and the whole family argued and fought and cried until bedtime.

Fortunately for Coal, he had inflicted considerable damage on his two white classmates, and the second day they left him alone. Thus he assumed a certain isolation, which his new teacher interpreted as the sullenness she had always associated with Negroes. But there would be other fights. Coal learned that a black boy his size was a coward if he didn't fight, a bully if he fought and won.

When basketball season began, the fighting continued, but now controlled by the rituals of the game. Elbows flew, feet reached out to trip, and scrambles for a loose ball on the floor resembled the struggle for life itself. But Coal's long arms flew farthest and hardest, and soon the other boys—black and white —granted him a grudging respect that extended at least the length of his elbows. With Coal's help, the grade-school team had its first winning season in years, and by February Coal had carved a place for himself. But at home, bitterness permeated the kitchen. Coal's father seemed more resentful that his son was making it in the white man's world than over his own failure in that world. In this climate, Coal's white dream grew.

By freshman year Coal was the biggest boy in the whole school, well over six feet tall. Nobody challenged him anymore, and he liked that. He saw white boys gazing at his naked size in the shower room, but he concealed his pride, saving their envy and fear for a time when they might be of use. Girls were attracted by his prowess and his handsome good looks, and not just colored girls. There was a story about Coal and a white cheerleader behind the bus barn after a game one night, and there was loose talk in a local bar about some "old-fashioned Southern justice." But nobody laid a hand on Coal.

By his senior year Coal was the local star. He led the Cougars to the first district championship in fifteen years. Several colleges came to see him play, and he was offered a scholarship to the state university. Everybody pleaded with Coal to take the offer—the coach, the principal, even his father. "What else can you do?" his father asked, swallowing any pride he had left. "You can't make no livin' sharecroppin' somebody else's farm." His mother cried when she begged him to go to school, told him it would break her heart if he turned it down. But Coal didn't go to college. He knew what he wanted to do.

The day after graduation Coal caught a ride into town. He went straight to the insurance office from which the red-faced landlord ran his growing empire. He swung open the door and strode right up to the boss's desk. "I want a job, Mr. Grabble," he said, looking straight into the puffy eyes. "I can do most anything."

The insurance man glared up from the papers on his desk, then shifted his bulk back in his swivel chair and chuckled. "Why, you're the Washington boy, aren't you?" he said. "I read about you in the paper. Offered a basketball scholarship? I'd think a colored boy'd jump at a chance like that. You know there's not even many white boys from these parts gets to go to college. Anyhow, I don't have a basketball team. What would you do for me?"

"I know how to farm, sir, and I'm strong, a good worker. I could manage some of your land."

Grabble laughed out loud. "Manage, you say? You mean you want to sharecrop like your old man, is that it?"

"No sir. I don't want to sharecrop. I'll work in your office here, or help arrange things with some of your black tenants, or whatever I can do to help you run your business."

Now Grabble didn't laugh. "Hmm," he said, nodding slightly. "You might have something there." Grabble thought of the dozen or so Negro tenants he had. They were always troubling him for one thing or another. Wanting more fertilizer, asking for an extension on their payments, expecting him to fix up the shacks he let them live in for free. And this boy knew them all. Grabble tore the cellophane off a big cigar and put it in his teeth. He chewed it thoughtfully for another moment, and suddenly he tipped his chair back forward, bringing his hands down flat on his desk. "You've got yourself a job," he said.

Thus began a process by which within a year Coal Washington had made himself indispensable to Jack Grabble. Any time there was a problem with a Negro tenant, Grabble sent Coal, and Coal always worked out a solution that was acceptable to his boss, and sometimes to the sharecropper as well. Coal came to know the details of Grabble's operation and his empire, as well as the financial affairs of his tenants. Coal was paid a modest salary, and he saved his money and waited. When Dred Mackey, the father of one of Coal's old classmates, was on the ropes, Coal was the first to know, and he paid Mackey a visit. By the time it got to Grabble, word had already spread throughout the black community that Coal had worked out a deal to buy the place, not for Grabble, but for himself.

Grabble was angry at first, and he almost threw Coal out. But he was impressed with the boy's shrewdness, and after second thoughts, he offered Coal a kind of partnership for the purchase and management of Negro land. "After all," Grabble told Coal, "most of these darkies wouldn't know what to do with a hundred dollars if they ever had it. They need somebody to help them manage their money, and that's where we come in."

By the time he was twenty-two Coal found himself in possession of over 200 acres of land, with three tenant farmers of his own. In November he dissolved his "partnership" with Grabble and walked out, leaving the landlord fuming. Coal gave his tenants notice that he would be farming the land himself, bought some used machinery, and was ready to plant by spring.

None of the houses on his three farms was fit to live in, so Coal hired an old classmate, a white man who was now a carpenter in town, to build him a house. They started after the fall harvest, working together, and by the dead of winter had put up the structure of what would be the biggest and fanciest house in the neighborhood. It had two bathrooms, like the houses Coal saw in the homebuilding magazines he read. Having huddled for years by a small, smoky woodstove, Coal had directed construction of a massive stone fireplace and hearth, and even though the carpenter advised that a cedar shingle roof and a wood burning fireplace could be a dangerous combination, Coal insisted on both.

When the house was finished in spring, Coal moved in alone, but already neighbors had seen him driving around the country in his new Ford with a young woman from Enid. That summer they were married, but Coal didn't take time for a honeymoon. He had just bought another farm, this time on borrowed money, an eighty that became available when Widow Barton died.

By now folks who had urged Coal to go to college were shaking their heads and smiling. "He knew what he wanted, that sly fox," they said. But some folks, both black and white, were not smiling. Some white neighbors, gazing across their fields at Coal's big house, began talking about "that uppity nigger." And some of the black folks were calling him "Junior Grabble" behind his back.

Coal was a relentless worker. His was the first light on in the morning, and the lights of his new tractor could be seen late into the night. The next fall he borrowed more money and bought yet another place, bought it from right under Grabble's nose. He now had so much land he couldn't work it all by himself, and he hired neighbor boys from time to time to help. Most didn't stay long. They said he worked them too hard and paid them too little. When they left they told stories about the arguments Coal had with his wife, and the Haley boy said he heard her scream one night when Coal went in and supper wasn't ready.

That was the year before Coal built the barn. He'd worked mostly alone that year, driving himself almost around the clock. Hardly ever did anybody catch the lights out at Coal's place. "At least he's not lazy," the neighbors had to admit.

It was while they were roofing the barn that his wife left. Coal and the carpenter were dragging heavy sheets of steel up to the rafters when she came out. Coal was straining and sweating, and he yelled at her to give him a hand. She tried to help, the carpenter remembered later, but there wasn't much she could do. So Coal began swearing at her, saying he should never have married a worthless city girl, that she was good for nothing outside of bed. Apparently she'd had enough, because she got in the Ford and left Coal watching from the barn roof as she drove away. She didn't return.

So that left Coal by himself with his big house and his big barn. Once a week or so his mother and his father, who were now over seventy and in poor health, would drive up in their rattletrap Chevy pickup. But other than that, Coal was alone.

The sun rose, and its dusty fingers inched down the haystack where Coal Washington slept. When the sun touched his eyes, they opened with a start. His first thought was that he hadn't slept this late in years and that he'd better get out of bed and get to work. Then he noticed the straw that covered him, and his crusted eyes focused on the rafters of the barn. Slowly it all came back. And still more slowly he raised his stiff body on his arms and gazed out the open hayloft door. Wisps of smoke still rose from the charred remains. A gentle gust lifted a swirl of ashes and carried them across the yard.

Coal lifted himself from the hay and dragged his aching body to the ladder. He lowered himself to the ground and climbed onto his tractor. He started the engine and raised the front-end loader. The tractor crawled out of the barn and across the yard to the smoldering ruin. Coal lowered the bucket and began pushing fallen timbers and burned furniture and all else that remained of his home into the cellar hole.

Coal was still at work when the deputy sheriff and Mr. Grabble, who still handled Coal's insurance, arrived. "Coal, get down off that tractor," Grabble ordered. "Don't you realize insurance won't pay for your loss if you destroy the evidence?"

For the first time in many months, Coal began to laugh. He had to stop the tractor to bring the heaving of his lungs under control. "Why Mr. Grabble," he gasped between laughs, "What do you mean, cover my loss? Why, I don't believe I took out the right policy, Mr. Grabble, sir. In fact, I'm not sure you got the kind of insurance that would cover my loss." Then he stopped laughing. "Now both of you get in that car and get off my land," he said calmly.

When the sheriff and the insurance man had gone, Coal finished the job. He shut off the engine, climbed down, and slumped in the ashes that had been his lawn, his back against the tire. He grasped his head between his knees, unable to contain the sobbing that shook his powerful frame.

THE ENDS OF THE EARTH

Tommy Mason's Chevrolet rumbled west, into the Oklahoma wind. The windows were down and the dusty spring air rushed across his face, drying salt streaks at the corners of his eyes. He concentrated on the glimmering asphalt that stretched away like a black serpent across the red earth toward Shawnee. "Just As I Am" from some radio church in Tulsa filled the spaces in the car, but not in his head. It was noon, and church would be getting out now—if they had it. He would be shaking hands, his stomach growling for another of Fanny Brighton's chicken dinners.

He was not shaking hands, but he was thinking about Fanny's chicken, about all those Sunday dinners for almost a year now, sometimes a pot roast, but almost always chicken, and always the best. And he was thinking about Fanny, wondering if Odell could actually believe he'd touched her in any way besides as a sister in Christ, or that he could have done what Odell claimed with any woman for that matter. But especially Fanny, her heavy body sagging on varicose legs, she almost old enough to be his grandmother.

There was nothing in Tommy's past to prepare him for this. His father had pastored little churches all over the western part of the state for over twenty years, and nothing like this had ever happened. Sure, Dimick was different in some ways. Most people in eastern Oklahoma were registered as Democrats, for example, but they voted for Nixon just the same, like the people Tommy knew back home. There were no blacks or Indians in Dimick; in McAlester and Holdenville yes, but not in Dimick. The people in the church were mostly retired farmers and coalminers, and none had any money to speak of. One of the deacons, Brother Spade, was a flat-earther who would argue all day that Jesus spoke literally when he said to take the gospel to the ends of the earth. This surprised Tommy a little at first, but he was glad that most of the congregation still believed that every word in the Bible is true.

Tommy's acceptance by these good folks was complete from the first. Some of his fellow ministerial students from the Baptist university had begun to let their hair grow, like hippies almost, but Tommy had his trimmed short every two weeks, just like his father. Though he was only twenty, Tommy had been respected in the church, and the few highschoolers who attended had followed his lead in the fight to keep dancing out of the school. He suspected that a couple of girls who embarrassed him with their penetrating gaze and more than sisterly hugs might have impure thoughts about him, but he carefully avoided being alone with them. Tommy could honestly say that his relationship, even with Shelley Bates, the cute senior who always wore short skirts and sat on the front pew, was purely spiritual.

Tommy rounded a curve and slowed down for Holdenville. He thought of the Cozy Diner, just past Sam's Surplus on the west end of town. Having missed Fanny's Sunday dinner, he wished he could stop for a Famous Chicken-Fried Steak, but he knew that was out of the question. He hadn't stopped there since the night a month back when they refused to serve Franklin Kingsley, and he wouldn't stop again. Their chicken-fries almost rivaled Fanny's cooking, but Tommy shook the dust from his feet as Jesus said to do when he and Franklin left that night, vowing aloud never to return.

It would be too late for lunch when Tommy got back to the dorm, so he weighed the other choices as the old Chevy clattered down Main Street, rejecting each place he passed as an unacceptable risk, either too dumpy, or more often too expensive, finally pulling in for a burger at the last place, the Tastee Freez across the highway from the Cozy Diner.

Tommy slid into a squeaky booth and glanced across the street at the diner's crowded parking lot. He was sure his hamburger would be inferior to other options that were no longer options, but he was hungry. That was one difference about this part of the state, he'd learned. Funny, he'd lived his whole life in Oklahoma and hadn't even known there were places where Negroes couldn't eat. He thought back to the towns in the west where he'd lived, Anadarko and Hobart and Guymon. He didn't remember many blacks in those towns, but there were Indians in at least two of them. He tried in vain to remember eating with Indians in the restaurants of those towns.

So Tommy's eyes were opened at the Cozy Diner. Now he saw the crowds from church going in, families in their Sunday best, more suits and ties than in Dimick for sure, people meeting and shaking hands before disappearing into the cool gleaming haven of Famous Chicken-Fried Steaks, all with one thing in common: all white.

Tommy thought about Franklin, who refused to make a scene about himself, realizing suddenly and with overwhelming outrage as they walked out that Franklin went quietly that night because he had done it so many times before, because he had learned, had accepted his second-class status. He had borne the insult because it was no longer an insult but only a way to survive. Tommy had wanted to yell at somebody, to let it be known that Franklin was a Christian gentleman and a man of God. He had burned to leave God's curse on the place for refusing one of his ministers. Indeed, Tommy had imagined turning over tables, breaking glasses, driving out the smug waitress and cashier who refused them, even as Jesus had driven the moneychangers from the temple. But Franklin had gone quietly to the car. He wasn't very hungry anyway, he said.

The only reason Franklin had been with Tommy in the first place was that it had been foreign missions week. The church headquarters in Oklahoma City had sent out a film about mission work in Africa, and the deacons had voted to take up a special collection to send medicine and food. That was when it occurred to Tommy to invite Franklin to speak. Franklin had never been to Africa, but he was black and a fellow ministerial student, and it seemed like a good idea at the time.

Tommy was still thinking about Franklin when the hamburger and French fries came. He remembered how they met, in freshman psychology the previous fall. It was a large class, and after two weeks of confusion about roll calls and seating, the professor, whose previous life as an elementary teacher had left her an unshakeable advocate of order, had assigned seats by alphabet. Tommy had never known a black person before, and he was glad that "L" came between Kingsley and Mason. There was bound to be at least one person in the class whose name began with "L." But somehow the professor had missed Kingsley, and had already seated Long and Martin and was up to Mason when Franklin raised his hand and politely informed her that he had been skipped. So Tommy and Franklin ended up side by side.

They hadn't spoken for the first two weeks of their accidental connection, but one day Tommy dropped his pen, and as he bent to pick it up Franklin did the same, and their hands touched. Franklin reached the pen first and handed it to Tommy with a smile. Tommy missed the rest of the lecture on human response, thinking about the smooth black hand with its shiny almost white palm, and the big flashing teeth. So before class a few days later they began to talk, and very slowly they became friends.

Foreign missions week was the first Sunday in April. Odell Brighton had missed church that day, the first time since Tommy became pastor in September. Fanny did come, but said she was sorry she couldn't have Tommy and Franklin for dinner. Odell was a little under the weather, she said. Several other regulars missed Franklin's talk too. Attendance was down from the usual fifty-five or sixty to about forty, even though it was Easter. Tommy showed the film, and Franklin talked about

Africa and the importance of sharing the Christian message with African people.

Since Odie Brighton was sick, Tommy and Franklin had driven down to McAlester for lunch at a barbecue place Franklin had heard about in the colored part of town. Tommy was a little tense eating with black people, but the barbecue was great.

On the way back to Shawnee after the evening service, just a mile or so out of Dimick, Tommy's left rear tire went flat. He wasn't surprised, since he'd been running on cord and air, and he even had a spare in the trunk, though unfortunately it wasn't mounted on a wheel. They tried to thumb for fifteen minutes, then gave up and walked all the way back to Dimick in the gathering darkness, one rolling the spare, the other the flat tire.

Only the Exxon was open on Sunday night. Tommy didn't know the guy on duty, a middle-aged man with a big belly and a bulbous nose. The man took one look at them and said he didn't change tires. "Then could we borrow your tools and change it ourselves?" Franklin asked. The attendant sprawled back in his chair and thought about it for a couple of big chews on his plug, spit in a coffee can, and said "I guess it's O.K., if you do it in the back. I don't want the regular customers to spot you."

Tommy and Franklin changed the tire, rolled the good one back to the Chevy and put it on, and headed on toward Shawnee. By then it was getting late and they were hungry, so they'd stopped at the Cozy Diner. That was when Tommy learned about restaurants that didn't serve blacks.

So that was Easter. On Thursday Tommy got a call from his mother that his grandpa was sick. He found a substitute for Sunday and headed out to the Panhandle. As it turned out, his grandpa had a stroke and died the following Thursday. So Tommy missed a week of school and two weeks in the pulpit. When he rolled back into Dimick, he sensed that something had changed, but he couldn't quite put his finger on it.

Tommy finished his burger and wiped the grease off his fingers and mouth. He paid his bill and headed back out into the grimy wind. He started the Chevy and backed out. He glanced across at the Cozy Diner once more as he pulled back onto the highway. He turned the radio up to compete with the wind, but the music wouldn't stop his mind from going over the whole morning again.

He'd arrived in Dimick a few minutes early, and had stopped for a roll and coffee at the Wagabag. Horace Littleton, the Sunday School superintendent, was putting gas in his pickup when Tommy came out, and Horace called him over. "I don't know if I'd show up at church this morning if I was you," Horace had told him. "Odell Brighton is pretty mad. He's told everybody in town about you and Fanny."

"What!" Tommy had stammered, totally surprised. "About what?"

"About your affair," Horace told him. "I don't know whether to believe it or not, what with her age and all, but most people seem to think there's something to it."

Tommy had been too flabbergasted to speak. He saw himself again, gripping the gas pump, his legs gone limp, his mouth hanging open in wonder. "There's one thing I know for sure," Horace flung over his shoulder as he turned his back and climbed into the truck. "You never should've brought that nigger here." Tommy clung to the gas pump like a cicada shell in a dry summer wind.

Another hour had passed when Tommy slowed down at the edge of Shawnee. He'd gone over the whole thing in his mind from beginning to end, three or four times, and it still made no sense. He relived driving up to the church in the warm April sun, remembered the brilliance of the lilies on the edge of the parking lot. He saw the row of cross-armed deacons standing elbow to elbow before the front door, their grim scowling faces locked on him. He felt again the long moment of indecision that was ten seconds and eternity, the Chevrolet in neutral, the engine rattling impatiently to go. He felt the stir conveyed by the last glimpse of Shelley Bates' saucy smile, the wink he was sure he saw through the crack in the door behind the deacons. He thought about the sermon he'd planned to give that morning on the theme of Christian brotherhood. Now he wondered if he'd ever preach that sermon, or any other for that matter, again. He didn't know. He was still too numb to tell.

The image of the phalanx of deacons faded again into Fanny Brighton's broad behind bent over the stove, turning fried chicken. He wondered most of all how Odell could have done that to her. But then for a moment he imagined Fanny with no clothes, the bulging blue veins running clear up to her sagging buttocks. He imagined doing what Odell Brighton told everybody in Dimick he did.

Suddenly Tommy was seized by a stroke of laughter which began in his head and seared like a high-voltage shock through his lungs and rumbled down through his body, clear to his toes on the gas pedal, swelling, shaking, quickly out of control. He swerved and hit the brakes and pulled the car off the road in front of Sid's Salvage, his sides shaking with anger and loathing and mirth and outrage and despair. Tears streamed down his face again, and his laughter roared out the open windows to merge with the Oklahoma wind.

THAT OLD-TIME RELIGION

For a couple of years Jake and Adrian rode only the south side, where Babe's had been. But eventually they rode the arbor side too, and one Saturday they stopped and looked the place over. Four years had passed since the crusade, and the roof had finally fallen in. But the walls still stood, and walking through the gap in the willow rails Adrian shuddered, remembering Sister Ruth and the night she scared the devil out of him and Jake.

They'd gone up early that night, in time to get a couple packs of Kool-Aid at Crookum's store before he closed. They were over at Babe's sucking it down and poking through what was left from the fire, waiting for the sun to set. They liked Kool-Aid mixed with sugar and water like everybody else, but it wasn't the same as taking it straight. Adrian's tongue curled around the powder. His eyes watered until the setting sun looked like a giant lollipop melting on Highway 29. His whole body shivered in the late August heat.

Jake wadded up his pack and tossed it in the weeds and raised up to read the sign again. " 'Sunset Crusade with Sister Ruth, 8:30 nightly.' I reckon it ought to be starting soon," he said. Adrian was just six and couldn't read, but Jake had finished third grade. Jake got up from a sooty concrete block and began prying at a piece of scorched wallboard to see what was underneath.

The boys lived a quarter mile down the road, and every time they picked through the trash they found something valuable that they'd missed before. Babe's Hilltop Lounge was a beer joint and dance hall that used to stand there, but all that was left was the foundation and a pile of burned-up rubble. Twisted bar stools, melted whiskey bottles, that sort of stuff. But the boys had also found a pile of melted quarters where the men's room used to be, a burned-up wrist watch that believe it or not still ticked, and inside the half-melted jukebox a bunch of warped and busted records. On one Jake made out the words "Oklahoma City," so he took a closer look and found "Count Basie" and "Blue Devil Blues." They even found a glass eye out of the moose that had hung on the wall. There was bound to be more good stuff buried in the ashes.

Babe's had burned down in May, right after the Oklahoma City woman got killed there. Jake and Adrian's dad said she was stabbed with a butcher knife out back in the parking lot, but the boys couldn't find any blood. Babe's burned on a Sunday morning. Lucky for them the pigs got out and they missed Sunday school, so they got to watch the fire.

It had been a big summer, what with the killing and the fire, and now Sister Ruth's revival meeting. Two men from Newalla had built the brush arbor, and it was mighty fine. They put up big blackjack posts for the corners, and used willows for rails around the sides and for rafters. On top they piled leafy willow branches, and they even made benches out of split logs. They practically cleaned out old man Roan's swamp. The boys had checked out the arbor just that afternoon on the way home from Crookum's, and it was peaceful and cool inside.

Mr. Crookum's gas station and store was across the Y from the arbor, kitty-cornered from Babe's. That's where the boys sold their bottles. They'd gotten into the bottle business in a pretty big way after berry season was over in June. Besides trapping gophers for the twenty-five-cent bounty on their tails, bottles were their main source of income. It was steady, and on a good day they cleared forty or fifty cents. Just about every bottle they found was worth two cents, so most days they made enough to each have a pop or an ice cream bar and still have money in their pockets.

The best picking was to the west, toward Okie City. Lots of folks out this way drove to work on Highway 29, and apparently had a cold pop on their way home. Lucky for them, most people didn't see the value in their bottles and just tossed them right out. At least once a week the boys headed west, riding the north ditch up to Baker's corner and the south ditch back home.

Adrian had bought his bike from Joe Gober for five bucks. The back tire was shot, and so was the gooseneck bearing, but it had a big basket in front that held even more bottles than the flour sack Jake tied to his handlebars. It was getting the bike after berry picking that put Adrian into business. Blackberries were good that year, and he made over eight bucks, so he had enough left for a new tire.

If they rode west on, say a Monday, they went east on Tuesday, sometimes as far as the Pott County line, which wasn't quite as good, but the good thing was they ended up at Crookum's on the way home. On days they wanted to laze around, maybe go crawdad fishing or catch frogs in the swamp, they'd take a quick spin north from the Y, or head south toward Newalla. Folks down toward Newalla were kind of stingy with their bottles, but the boys found lots of other good stuff in a dump by the creek on that run, like once they found a whole sack of cookies with only a couple eaten, and another time they found a spotlight off a car. Jake wired it to his handlebars and it really dressed up his bike.

Anyhow, it had been a pretty good summer, and Adrian didn't want it to end. He had to start first grade in a week, and he wasn't sure he wanted to go. But Sister Ruth was bound to put some spark in his last week of freedom. Mr. Crookum said she was one of the most famous evangelists in the state, and a real ball of fire. He said that was one show he didn't want to miss.

Just then a car pulled up to the arbor, a Nash Jake said it was, and four women got out. They wore long dark dresses and had their hair piled up on their heads. Jake and Adrian crouched down behind Babes' foundation to watch, thinking at first that one of them might be Sister Ruth. The sun was sinking over the hill beyond their house, and they could see a dim light in the kitchen window, where likely their mother was washing the supper dishes. They'd told her they were going down the creek to catch bullfrogs.

More cars pulled off the highway, mostly beat-up old cars, one just like their '41 Ford. They saw that most of the men were in short sleeves, but one carload had suits and ties and stuff like that. These guys opened the trunk, and careful like they were gathering eggs, they lifted out a big shiny pulpit and carried it in. People milled around in the dusk, and some, mostly women, went on into the arbor. But the guys in suits came back out and stood in a knot with their heads bowed down, praying, Adrian figured. Ever once in a while, a "Praise Jesus!" or the like came floating across Highway 29.

It was getting darker, so the boys eased up and stretched their necks so as to see better. That was a mistake, because no sooner had they stuck up their heads than one of the preachers spotted them and motioned with his arm. "Come on over and meet the Lord, boys," he called. Adrian and Jake looked at each other, wondering whether to hide or run, but it was too late to do either. The guy pulled away from the crowd and came loping across the highway to Babe's. "Come on over and hear Sister Ruth, boys," he said in a kindly voice. A big hand gripped each of their collars, and he herded them toward the arbor. What could they do but go?

Now the arbor was pretty near full, and still no Sister Ruth. A fat woman on the front row shot the boys a toothless grin and scooted down the sagging willow bench to make room. And wouldn't you know it, this preacher led them in and set them down not ten feet from the pulpit.

They'd no sooner sat down than a big commotion swept through the crowd. They stretched up and saw a shiny red car pulling up in front, a Buick, Jake said. The flock of preacher lookers rolled right over to the passenger side, practically tripping over each other to get to the door. Out steps a big blonde woman, near six feet tall, in a slick green dress and her hair rolled up on top of her head like the others, but like she just stepped out of the beauty shop. It was Sister Ruth.

Sister Ruth strode right up to that polished pulpit, the crowd parting for her like hens when a rooster comes through. She looked to be about forty, and she flashed a mouthful of shiny teeth when she laughed and greeted the crowd, several by name as Sister this or Brother that. She had a big black Bible in her right hand, and she held it high to the cheering crowd. Adrian began to see what Mr. Crookum meant, though he hadn't spotted him anywhere in the crowd.

Sister Ruth sat down on a chair with a big fluffy cushion, and one of the preacher guys got up in front to lead the singing. They didn't have any song books, but they didn't seem to need any. Adrian and Jake even knew one of the songs, "Are You Washed in the Blood?" though they hadn't heard it sung with that much spunk before. After the singing and some praying, the preachers took up a collection in two-quart shortening cans. Then it was Sister Ruth's turn.

By now the arbor was full to busting. There was a dim light bulb hanging in every corner, and a brighter one right over the pulpit, so the boys could see everything pretty well. Sister Ruth stood up, cleared her throat, and started out slow, in a voice that sounded almost like a man. "Brothers and sisters," she began, "I've come out from Tulsa this evening because there's a burden on my heart. The Lord spoke to me last week, and he said, Sister Ruth, there's sinners down Newalla way that need to be freed from the Devil's grip. There's folks down there cryin' tonight because they don't know where to turn, and they need mercy. Mercy!" she said again, louder. "Mercy!" she shouted out, and the branches overhead began to shake. Adrian spotted a furry caterpillar on a willow leaf, inching like mad toward the back of the arbor.

"These sinners don't need justice," Sister Ruth said. "Justice would send them to burn forever in fire and brimstone. They need mercy!" She was getting warmed up and began to holler in a kind of chant, her voice rising and wailing. And just when Adrian thought she'd reached the top of her lungs, she'd yell even louder. "Not justice, Lord! What they deserve is a Devil's Hell. But mercy! They need mercy! Mercy! Mercy!"

Adrian glanced past Sister Ruth over to the charred remains of Babe's, remembering the roaring fire licking through the roof, eating the walls, whiskey bottles busting in the crackling flames. He remembered the Blue Devils on the busted record, and the awful heat that drove Jake and him and the other watchers back and back from the blaze. Ten feet away, Sister Ruth raged on, and he felt the fire again.

"I know out there tonight there's a man who's a slave to the bottle," Sister Ruth said. "There's a woman who's covered the face God gave her with lipstick and rouge to tempt men to lust after her. There's a young girl here who's disobeyed her father. Somewhere in this crowd there's a boy who's cheated or stole, who's lied to his dear mother, who might die tonight and go as sure to eternal fire as the drunkard or the loose woman. God, this man, this woman, this girl, this boy don't need justice, they need mercy! Mercy! Mercy!" Sister Ruth screamed, and her eyes lit right on Adrian.

Adrian was beginning to sweat, and it wasn't just the August heat. He was remembering the time he and Jake snatched bottles of grape pop off the truck while the driver was in Crookum's. The bench shuddered, and in the corner of his eye he saw the fat woman bawling like somebody died. She was banging on the willow slab with her fist and crying for mercy. He twisted around and saw other folks jumping up, some beginning to shudder and sway and shout. "Yes, Sister! That's me, Sister!" somebody yelled. "Preach on, Sister. Praise the Lord"!

A few folks looked happy, but most were weeping and wailing. Some were on their knees in the dust between the benches, and one woman passed out cold in the aisle. Adrian and Jake's folks took them to church most Sundays, and they'd been to their grandparents' country church on the Cimarron River, but neither place had ever been like this. It seemed the shouts and cries and pleas would blow the brush right off the arbor roof.

Adrian glanced at Jake, and he was paler than when he came home from school with the measles. Adrian figured Jake was remembering the fire too, and maybe thinking about the pop, or the time Mr. Crookum gave him a dime too much and he didn't say a word.

Well, this went on for what seemed like an hour, getting louder and more out of hand by the minute. By now Sister Ruth was downright raving. Somebody puked in the back, and people were crying out in strange-sounding languages Adrian had never heard. Adrian was scared. He could tell by his looks that Jake was scared too, not only of Hell and the Devil and eternal fire, but of Sister Ruth and this whole crowd. Adrian had never seen people this worked up before, not even people staggering out of Babe's the night he and Jake sneaked out of bed after midnight and went to the edge of the woods to watch.

Then Sister Ruth shouted with a voice louder than anything they'd heard before that they must pray, pray for forgiveness for their miserable lives, pray for mercy. Most of the crowd dropped in the dust and clung to those willow benches like a flock of cicadas, sobbing and crying to be spared from hell. Jake and Adrian crouched down on their knees too. Jake's face was white in the glare from the bulb over Sister Ruth. "Let's get out of here," he whispered in a voice like a stuck frog's.

How?" Adrian asked, eyeing the double rail that ran around the edges of the arbor. There was just one opening, right behind the pulpit, and Sister Ruth had that covered. She was really working the crowd now, her long legs carrying her back and forth across the front. Half a dozen steps from the pulpit to the wall, she'd turn and stomp back, eyeing the boys each time through. She pounded the pulpit on her way by, then paced to the other side and back again. Getting through that gap wouldn't be easy.

"Get ready to run," Jake whispered over the shouting and crying and moaning and pleading. "When she passes the door, we go," he said, so cool that Adrian thought they might actually make it. "When she gets back, we'll be gone."

Sister Ruth paused in mid-stride to strike the pulpit, then she was off again, each step in beat with a cry for mercy. She passed the opening, took four steps west to the rail, and turned. Four strides brought her back to the door and then beyond. "Now!" yelled Jake, a lot louder than had to be.

Up off the dusty earth they leapt. Past the pulpit, and out the gap in the wall they streaked, their shrieks of panic and escape mixed with the jumbled roar from the arbor. They dodged through parked cars and ripped across the highway without checking for traffic. Adrian heard tires scream before he saw the headlights, and jumped clear just as a car skidded by. From the corner of his eye he glimpsed Babes' dark foundation, where the Devil likely lurked. Down the hill they fled, screaming all the way, pursued by Satan and Sister Ruth.

When they turned up the driveway at last, their mother stood by the porch light, her hand shading her eyes, squinting for them in the shadows. Adrian glanced back once as they crossed the creek, and saw only darkness behind. They slowed to a panting trot as they entered the feeble circle of light, which spread out from their waiting mother like a gleaming halo.

DESIRE AND SHIFTING SAND

The screen door slammed, and without a word Rudolph Seeborg shuffled across the linoleum to the living room. He flipped on the TV, unstrapped his overalls, sprawled in the faded mohair chair and tugged at his brogans. In the kitchen, Ethel hunched over the woodstove, warming leftover biscuits and beans.

The black-and-white image was fuzzy with snow, but Rudolph recognized Goon Wrangler, his favorite wrestler. Goon was having a field day with Fats Checker, pounding him into the ropes. "Hit him again!" Rudolph yelled, and he slashed the air with the shoe he had just removed. "Harder!" Rudolph swung again, and almost toppled onto the floor. Fats recovered and kicked Goon square in the belly. Goon hit the deck hard, bounced, and was back on his feet. He charged like a raging bull, burying his head in Fats' fat middle, splattering sweat through the snowy waves. "You got him!" Rudolph cried. He swung again, and the brogan slipped from his fingers, ricocheted off the pot-bellied stove, and careened into a pile of sleeping cats in the corner. Cats squalled and spat and leapt for the screen door.

"Turn that damn thing off, Rudy," Ethel hollered from the kitchen. "Ain't you got nothin' better to do than watch those slobs smash each other into sausage? I told you the calf was out again this morning. And you know that hay's not gonna bale itself. Somebody's got to get some work done or the banker's gonna be sniffin' around here again like a bull after a heifer."

"Who's not working?" Rudolph demanded sullenly from the door frame. "To hell with this farm! What fool ever thought a man could make a living on eighty acres of worn-out sand anyhow? And if you're looking for complaints, Rosie's going dry too. The hay's got more crabgrass than Sudan, and the only place it ever rains is through the holes in the barn roof." Rudolph struck the TV switch with his open palm.

"Fifty years I put in this place, Ethel, and I got about as much as I come here with. Why, there's coloreds down the road got more than I got. And now they're striking oil all over the country, but do you s'pose we'll get a well? Fat chance. That'd be too much to ask. Hell, I'll go to my grave with no more to show for a life of hard work than a blown-out eighty and a stinking outhouse!" Rudolph's heart was beating fast, and the pink flowers on the linoleum blurred and began to shift. He'd been feeling better, but now the headache was returning, and sweat formed on his brow. He gripped the kitchen door and clinched his eyes.

"Now settle down, Rudolph," Ethel warned. "You're workin' yourself up to another stroke, and Lord knows we cain't afford no more doctor bills. Just set yourself down and eat some biscuits and beans and you'll feel better."

Rudolph slumped into a creaky chair at the kitchen table, and Ethel sat down across the checkered oil cloth. "I don't know why I ever stayed in this sand country anyhow," he resumed. "I could have gone to California in the thirties like everybody else with any sense. But no, I had to stay here with the darkies, waiting for the next dust storm to suffocate the cows, waiting for the banker to come around for his money, waiting for the sheriff to try to sell me out. Now I'm watching everybody else get oil. Hell, even the coloreds are getting rich, and I can't even fix the barn roof."

"Now you just hush," Ethel said. "There's no call to go blamin' yourself." Rudolph nibbled at a biscuit. He wondered why she'd married him anyway, old as he was. She'd done her part, even working in the field beside him, trying to make something of the place. But she knew as well as he did how little they'd gained for their work. "Yes," she agreed after a bit, "an oil well would be nice." Rudolph choked down his bitterness with a gulp of water and began to eat. He chewed the hard biscuits and beans slowly. When dinner was over, it would be back to work.

When he finished, Rudolph struggled up from the table and filled a quart jar at the sink. At least they had good cool water. He wrapped the jar in last week's Cimarron Clipper, and tied it with a scrap of baler twine. There was a story on the front page about three new wells in the county, one of them a gusher. He put on his crumpled straw hat and hobbled out into the scorching Oklahoma sun. The putt-putt-putt of pumping oil wells echoed the pulse in his temples.

Rudolph put the old Ford in third and started down the lane, the baler jangling rhythmically behind. To the west he could see the horse's head rising and dipping on the Watsons' well. At least the tractor drowned out the beat. How lucky can you get, he thought. In the county seven years, and the Watsons had struck it rich. Probably have the farm paid off in a couple of years, and he still had a mortgage after twenty. Twenty years for eighty acres, and all the good land on the place about enough to dig a grave. He couldn't help glancing east. He could almost see old Cotter's toothless black face, grinning over all that oil.

Rudolph pulled into the little field and angled up to the first windrow. He kicked the power take-off in and eased out the clutch. With a groan, the baler's plunger scraped and slammed and gathered speed. Immediately a cloud of powdery dust engulfed him, grit drifting into his nostrils and eyes. He blinked at the dust, and tears seeped from his eyes. He gasped for air, choked, and sprayed brown saliva. He gripped the wheel and stood up on the clutch. He closed his eyes until the foul cloud passed.

He dug in his overalls pocket for a bandana, mopped his face and tied the cloth around his nose. The field was not large, but he couldn't hold his breath the whole downwind stretch. He surveyed the windrows, and figured if he didn't break down he might be done in an hour. His head was throbbing now, and his dust-filled eyes wouldn't quite focus. At dinner he'd thought it was just the heat, but now he wasn't so sure. The blistering sun transformed the field into a shimmering sea, and the windrows of hay seemed to roll like waves. He averted his gaze to the tiny pool of shade beside the tractor, and after a moment the brown stubble stood still, each stalk distinct. He gripped the wheel and squinted straight down the windrow. He let up the clutch, and the field was in motion again, he like a banking hawk in a dust storm.

At last he reached the corner and bore down on the brake, turning south, free of the blinding cloud. He wiped his eyes on his sleeve and strained to look back. The last two bales sprawled like busted accordions behind him. He stopped the Ford and crawled down to ease the tension on the baler. The hot sand burned through the soles of his shoes. He drank from the water jar and climbed back on the tractor.

From his overalls bib he withdrew a cellophaned plug of Red Man. He bit off a chunk and put the rest away. He slipped the tractor back into second and headed down the row. The posts were barely visible in the sand-drifted fence. This year wasn't as dry as the thirties, but it was bad enough. Rudolph bounced over a gopher hole, arrived at another corner and turned west, lulled by the steady thud, thud, thud of the baler's plunger. A streak of thick brown juice mingled with the sweat and dust on his chin.

There were half a dozen rounds to go when he spotted the old green International crawling down the lane. The Watson boys were right on time. Pretty good boys, those Watsons. Hard-working, dependable, not like most kids these days. But he'd better keep an eye on them anyway. Probably better pay them by the bale instead of the hour, just to be sure. The truck lurched to a stop in a cloud of dust, and three wiry teenagers, naked and brown from the jeans up, got out to wait for Rudolph to finish his round.

"Howdy, boys," Rudolph called from the tractor. "You can get right to work. I want the bales stacked in the chicken house. It's got a better roof than the barn. And be careful not to break any. You have to eat all you break." The boys laughed and put on their gloves. Junior, who was barely tall enough to see over the dash, slid behind the wheel and turned down the first row, Jake pitching and Adrian stacking the bales.

Round and round Rudolph rode, the dusty eastern stretch marking the rounds. Every circuit was smaller than the one before, and the hot shoe of his right brake stank from frequent turns. He was almost finished now, but his headache was getting worse. The tractor crawled steadily along, but he couldn't shake the feeling that it was he who was stationary, and the field that moved round and round below the wheels. But he kept going, struggling with this unsettling perception for the last two windrows, and then he was done. He killed the Ford, climbed down, and slumped in the shade of the rear tire.

He took off his straw hat and mopped his forehead with the bandana. He felt the deep crease from the hatband that marked the break from the dusty leather of his face to the delicate white of his balding head. He bit off another hunk of Red Man and waited for the Watson boys to finish. He would leave the baler in the field in case more bales broke.

The steady growl of the International and the rhythmic cracking of his cooling engine weren't enough to drown out the putt, putt, putt, roll, putt, putt, putt, roll of old Cotter's well, pumping away across the fence. Sometimes the wind brought a faint out-of-time echo from the Watsons' well. The round-the-clock rhythm of the pumps, which recently he'd begun to feel even in his sleep, pulsed with the life blood of money and luck and ease, the thumping heart of a coveted beast, the beat and the smell of which haunted every waking moment and even troubled his dreams. The cadence had persisted unbroken for six months now, the bitter salt smell of crude oil permeating every breath. Now, slouched in the shade of the tractor tire, the throb of the one-lunged engines merged with the throb in his head, and the image of the bobbing horse's head would not leave his mind. Rudolph concentrated on the wind and tried to shut out the other sounds.

When the load was five bales high, Jake took the wheel and the battered truck groaned and crawled to the center where Rudolph waited. The door screeched open and the boys squeezed over to make room for him. Rudolph hobbled through the dust and pulled himself up on the running board. He collapsed on the springy seat and slammed the door.

"How's your well pumping?" Rudolph asked as they bounced out of the field.

"Good," said Jake. "Dad says maybe I can get me a car next year."

"Those girls in town better look out!" Rudolph said. He laughed, and pain stabbed at his eyes. He hung his head out the window and spewed tobacco juice. "I guess I'll never see any of that oil," he complained. "The only hole they'll ever dig on this place will be to put me in." He pinched his eyes to squeeze out the pain. At least being with the boys made him feel a little better. Though Ethel had a grown son in Tulsa who visited once or twice a year, Rudolph had no children of his own, and he liked having the boys around. He entertained them with stories, like when he used to shoot coyotes through the open windshield of a '28 Chevy, steering down rutted trails with one hand, firing a 22 rifle with the other. Coyotes were so thick in those days, he said, that folks decorated their Christmas trees with tails.

When the boys were younger, he and Ethel always counted on them for Halloween. The only other neighbor in walking distance was Widow Barton, a woman so old she couldn't tell Halloween from Christmas Eve. They tried her the first year they lived here, creeping through her dark yard as a ghost, a pirate, and a corpse. They scared the old lady so bad Rudolph heard her scream a quarter mile away, and she raved about evil spirits for weeks. So that left only Rudolph and Ethel, who always bought plenty of candy and had as much fun feigning horror as the boys had inflicting it. He recalled the time they brought the black cat. In the breeze of the truck window he was feeling a little better.

"Say, did I ever tell you about the cat I couldn't get rid of?" Rudolph asked.

"Not that I recall," Jake lied.

"Well, this cat got to killing chicks, so I had to get rid of it. First I shot the cat and left it for dead. But next morning the thing was waiting like usual on the doorstep. Next day I fed the beast enough rat poison to kill a dog. But by evening she'd recovered, seemed stronger than ever. So on the third day I cut the old girl's head off and dumped her body in the woods. But sure enough, next morning there was that cat standing on the porch, holding its head in its mouth." The boys laughed almost as much as Rudolph did, but laughing intensified the pounding behind his eyes.

They pulled into the yard and Jake carefully backed the truck up to the chicken house door. Rudolph was glad he was too old to buck bales. He sure wouldn't want to stuff hay in a hell hole like that, not in this heat. Besides, the ache had spread back through his head now, and into his neck. He thought he could actually hear the throbbing. He felt for the door handle and pulled and slid to the ground. He squinted past the barn toward old Cotter's well, but it wouldn't hold still. "I think I'll set down in the shade and rest a spell," he told the boys. "This heat's about to get me."

Rudolph hobbled to the big elm and turned up a five-gallon grease bucket to sit on. Through the blurred kitchen window he saw Ethel at the sink, probably fixing sandwiches for the boys. Three chickens pecked idly at something on the porch of the little house. Rudolph noticed how deeply the roof was sagging.

Instead of feeling better in the shade as he'd hoped, he felt worse by the minute. Too damn old to be working in this heat, he thought, but what else could he do if he wanted to eat? He wished Ethel would come out and bring him a cold drink from the well. Maybe he should go in the house and lie down, but sure as he did those boys would take a break. So he cradled his head in his hands and shifted his stocky frame, trying to get comfortable.

After a bit, he glanced toward the house again. Ethel was still at the window. She ought to bring him some water. He raised his hand and tried to wave. A shock streaked through his body, arching his back. His head jerked back against the elm, knocking off his hat. He grabbed for the tree but caught only air, the grease can tipping one way and he the other, sprawling on his back in the dry sand. His head hit a root and lolled toward the house. The chickens, Ethel, and the window disappeared.

Rudolph opened his tortured eyes and looked up into the tree. Why was he lying in the dirt? He rolled his head toward the barn. The boys had finished unloading and were dunking and splashing in the stock tank, washing off sweat and crabgrass dust. He heard a rumble, and from the south a column of dust was rolling up the road, chasing a big black car. It slowed as it approached, and turned in to the driveway. It came to a stop just outside the circle of shade.

Rudolph rolled his head toward the blinding sun and the gleaming automobile. His eyes squinted at the shimmering chrome. A dusty door opened, and the driver got out. He was tall, wearing a dark suit and a cowboy hat and boots. Striding like a banker in a barnyard, the big stranger ambled over to the shade. His suit had pinstripes, and even a handkerchief folded in the breast pocket.

"Howdy," the man said. "Mr. Seeborg? Taking a little nap, are you? I'm Red Crosser with Richstrike Drilling. Come out to talk about looking for oil on your place." A big freckled hand reached out to Rudolph where he lay on the ground. From the accent the guy sounded like Texas, and Rudolph wondered vaguely why his name was Red, since the hair sticking out below his hat was brown. But oil! Didn't the guy say oil? For an instant, instead of the Texan, Rudolph saw himself sitting in the shade on his front porch, rocking in time with a big black oil pump just beyond the yard fence. He sipped iced lemonade, and his overalls were clean.

Rudolph refocused on the stranger and gathered his strength to get up. He hesitated, then extended his own horny hand, and the other man took it. The big hand pulled and Rudolph heaved his body forward, but his grip failed and he staggered, falling back against the tree. The Texan disappeared in another wave of blackness.

When the stranger came back, the big hand was still there. Eyeing the shiny boots and the pinstriped pants, Rudolph slowly reached again. The Texan took his hand and all but lifted him from the ground and set him on his bucket, just as the Watson boys came dripping from behind the trunk of the elm. "Yes sir, Mr. Seeborg," the Texan was saying, "You're going to be a rich man. Our tests show there's lots of oil under your place. What do you say, old man. Ready to sign?"

Rudolph's eyes followed the stripes up to the beige cowboy hat, which became the dusty leaves of the elm. He tried to blink things clear, but the Texan and the boys and the big car and even Cotter's oil well had begun to swirl and spin together, and his throbbing head was ready to burst. "Oil?" he managed to squeak. "Rich, did you say? Sign? Where are the papers?"

Then a flood of blackness that Rudolph could not resist washed through his thick body and crashed like sorrow in his head. The blackness of the suit and the car and the well merged with the bigger blackness, and he lurched forward from his can, grabbed at nothing, and reeled face down to the earth. He opened his eyes again against the blackness. "Oil," he said. Then his eyes closed, and rich brown juice seeped from the corner of his mouth into the sand.

MOONLIGHTING

"Sure, I'll give you boys a job. Two bucks an hour, and you can start right now." Pick Picklesimer sprawled back in his swivel chair and scratched dead skin off his left ear. "You can take the '53 Chevy, but don't push her too hard. And put in a quart of oil before you go." He finished scaling his ear and launched himself on screeching springs back to his desk. He hoisted his belly and grabbed a sweaty Stetson off the filing cabinet. "Come on. I'll show you what's ready to go."

Bart and Adrian trailed Picklesimer out of the musty little office into the "showroom," down a dirty zigzagging aisle between stacks of dusty TVs and stereos, past sagging beds and sad chests of drawers and chrome dining tables and chairs, to the slightly brighter front of the store where couches and chairs and lamps and coffee tables were arranged in crooked rows and piles. There were even a few nearly matched sets. "Take this couch and chair," he said, delivering a moderate kick to an ancient brown mohair that raised a decades-old cloud of dust. He tested the varying degrees of instability of several veteran coffee tables, finally settling on what looked like the worst of the lot. "Throw this in, too. 2125 Patton Boulevard. A Mrs. Gonzo, a real cutie. She's already paid, so don't try to collect in merchandise," he said with a wink. He turned and maneuvered his bulk back through the obstacle course toward his office.

Adrian jiggled the coffee table on its legs and busted out laughing. "I can't believe we're doing this," he said as Picklesimer disappeared into his air-conditioned sanctum.

"Especially not for two bucks an hour."

"Hey," said Bart, "for two bucks an hour he gets two bucks' work, right?" He went out to find the '53, and Adrian started scooting furniture toward the front door.

They lugged Mrs. Gonzo's furniture into the back of the truck, and they were off in a cloud of blue smoke. It was only later that they remembered the boss had told them to check the oil.

It didn't take long to find the recipient of these treasures. Patton is the main drag through beautiful downtown Killeen, which lies smack in the armpit of Fort Hood, Texas. Toward the far end of town, Patton narrowed and trailed off into rows of tiny derelict houses, beat-up trailers, and a two-block stretch of World War II barracks some double-dipper hauled off the base and partitioned for apartments. Their friend Al and his wife Suzy lived there, so Adrian and Bart knew how elegant they were. Three small rooms with leaky faucets, cracked windows, and chipping plaster for a hundred bucks a month.

Al was a PFC like Adrian and Bart, but being married, he got a housing allowance which doubled his take to over two hundred. So after taxes and rent, Al and his new bride had about ninety dollars left for gas, clothes, furniture, food, and all the other luxuries of life. Quite a honeymoon Al was having. But the situation was tolerable, the Army apparently figured, since it was only temporary. They'd all be in 'Nam in a few months anyway, and then Al would have other things to worry about besides whether his wife was comfortable.

"Upstairs, wouldn't you know it?" Bart grumbled as he backed the truck up to 2125. They went up to find Mrs. Gonzo. Probably she didn't hear them knocking for awhile because of all the screaming, but she finally opened the door. "Shut up, Bobby," she yelled over her shoulder at a diapered toddler with snot dripping off his chin.

"Yes?" she asked.

"Furniture City," Adrian said. "We've brought your couch and chair."

"Oh. Bring it on up," she said, brightening. She picked up the kid, who gawked at Bart and Adrian and forgot why he was bawling. She started shoving boxes out of the way with her foot, making room for the couch. Her dumpy bottom was crammed into red-and-white striped shorts, and her hair was in rollers. The delivery team headed back down the stairs, dodging a mop bucket and a snarl of toys.

They lugged the couch up first, gouging walls and busting their guts forcing it around the corner at the top. They heaved the monstrosity against the wall and collapsed on it, sending another cloud of Texas soil whooshing up around their heads.

"That's not the one I rented," Mrs. Gonzo said flatly. "It was green, and not so . . . ratty. At ten dollars a month you'd think he'd give me the right one. My husband sends just enough for the rent, and sometimes not even that, and I don't think . . . " Her lip quivered and tears pooled in her eyes. As if in sympathy, the baby resumed his howl.

"Look, lady," Bart said, whiny but not altogether unkind, "we just do what we're told. And that thing's too heavy to take back down those stairs. You'll have to take it up with Picklesmoker."

"Picklesmoker, that's funny," Mrs. Gonzo said with a little laugh, and for the first time Adrian saw there was something slightly cute about her face. "I guess it'll have to do," she sighed, dabbing at her eyes. "Go ahead and bring up the rest."

The rest of Mrs. Gonzo's suite went up easier, and soon they were roaring back down Patton, followed by the cloud of smoke. "Whew, that was a drag," said Bart. "That calls for a beer." He pulled off at the Horseshoe and parked the '53 out of sight in back. They went in for a cool tap, figuring they'd already earned their two bucks for that hour.

When they came out, the sun was getting low, but it was still hot. With a softened perspective on their new job, they climbed in and rattled on down Patton toward Furniture City. They calculated their prospects, concluding that if they worked four hours every evening after their Army jobs they could each make an extra forty bucks a week. Not big money exactly, but almost twice what Uncle Sam was paying them, and cash to boot. In a couple of weeks they'd have the resources for a bombshell weekend in Nuevo Laredo.

It was in the midst of their calculations that they became aware of a knocking under the hood. Adrian glanced back and saw that their volume of smoke had doubled. The oil pressure needle was bouncing on zero. "Park this beast," Adrian said. "We're out of oil."

Bart pulled over, and the engine died with a clunk. Adrian scrounged through the trash under the seat and pulled out two cans of Quaker State. He poured them in, and they were off again, the blue haze back to normal.

"What in Sam Hill took you so long?" Picklesimer demanded when they walked in. It was getting dark and he was waiting to close. "I wanted you to make another delivery."

"The lady claimed you sent the wrong set," Bart answered. "It took awhile to smooth her feathers, but between the two of us we managed." He flashed Picklesimer a conspiratorial grin, and the boss's scaly face relaxed, and then he laughed.

"Why you sly devils," he said with a red-palmed slap to Bart's back. "She was a cutie all right, wasn't she?" Then he was all business again. "There's one more delivery that has to be made tonight. I promised it for last week and she's getting impatient. It's just a TV," he added, leading them back to what he called the "home entertainment section."

They started their new job on Monday. They worked every evening that week, delivering an endless motley array of worn-out beds and couches and TVs to a seemingly endless supply of privates and PFCs and wives whose husbands had been shipped to Vietnam. Likely as not, what they delivered was not what folks had selected in Picklesimer's showroom. Sometimes the lady made a fuss, and a couple of times the boys actually hauled the merchandise back and exchanged. But usually, customers weren't too surprised to get less than they'd bargained for. Their status on the bottom rung of the military ladder had accustomed them to ripoffs and abuse. Anyway, most of them figured it was only for a couple of months, so why bother?

What particularly upset two or three different parties that week was the same old G.E. console TV they kept delivering from one dump to another. The best it would produce for ten bucks a month was a rolling blizzard through which an image mysteriously flashed for a split second with each revolution. Presumably Picklesimer figured folks would be too worn out to notice. But he underestimated how seriously some people take their TV.

Bart and Adrian delivered this revolving box of junk for the third time on Friday to a pretty young thing out in Courtly Cove. That's a little town west of Fort Hood where people who could afford someplace besides Killeen lived. This gal was married to a sergeant who was off to war, and he'd been gone too long. She was wearing the same cute miniskirt and tight blouse they'd seen her in when she came to the store. And she was all dolled up, like she was expecting them.

They dragged the old clunker into her living room and plugged it in, hoping to clear out before she turned it on. But then she offered them a beer, and of course they couldn't say no. She and Bart sat down on her genuine Picklesmoker couch, and Adrian sat across the room where he'd have the best view of her legs. She quickly forgot about the T.V., and so did Bart. Before they finished the beers, she'd scooted clean over to Bart's end, and he had his arm around her. Feeling awfully sorry for himself, Adrian offered to go out for more beer.

He fired up the '53 and drove downtown. He went to the Rattlesnake, which was about what he felt like, and took a stool at the end of the bar. He had two beers by himself, and once he even thought about Picklesmoker, wondering if he'd tired of waiting for them and gone home. But mostly he thought about those legs and wished he'd grabbed the couch first.

About nine, Adrian bought a six-pack and headed back over to her house. The full moon was just coming up. When he got there, Bart had a big honey-licking grin on his face, and the woman was bubbling like a glass of champagne. He was on the floor by the TV, trying to get the picture to hold still, pretending they hadn't already delivered the monstrosity twice that week, that he had no idea it wasn't in prime condition.

They had another beer, and Bart said they'd take the tube back to Picklesmoker for a tune-up. She agreed right away, probably thinking about another delivery. So they lugged the junker back out to the truck. She kissed them both goodnight, which made Adrian feel even more like a flat spare tire. Bart got her phone number, and the boys headed back toward Killeen, Adrian behind the wheel.

"You know, Bart," Adrian said when they got out of town, "I don't think I can take this job anymore."

Bart looked surprised. "Well, I know the pay's not the best," he said. "But I do like the fringe benefits." And the sucker laughed out loud.

"Yeah," Adrian said, "but I can't take any more of Picklesmoker and his flaky face and his lies and his junk couches and TVs."

There's one big curve in an otherwise straight road between Courtly Cove and Killeen, and it was coming up. They'd never pushed the Chevy beyond about fifty, partly out of respect for its condition, and mostly because at two bucks an hour they'd never been in a hurry. But now Adrian stomped the gas pedal to the floor.

Groaning and clattering, the old truck picked up speed. Fifty-five, sixty, sixty-five. The engine rattled and roared, and he could see the trail of smoke in the moonlight. "Hey, you'd better slow this baby down," Bart said, a tinge of anxiety in his voice. But Adrian didn't let up. They were just over seventy when the headlights found the curve sign ahead. Bart gripped the vibrating dash as the truck veered into the bend. The tires began to squeal and the steering wheel shimmied. Adrian kept his foot to the floor until he heard the TV begin to scoot. He watched in the mirror as it hit the wall of the bed with a bang, rose on two legs, danced for a beautiful second in the moonlight, and was gone. The big box exploded on the moonlit shoulder, wood and glass and tubes shattering, disintegrating, airborne, disappearing into the darkness of the deep bar ditch. A fit of laughter seized Adrian and spread to Bart, and they and the Chevy roared through the hot Texas night, the insistent hammering of the out of oil engine barely audible over their howls of glee.

"Wouldn't you love a glimpse of Picklesmoker's face if he could've seen that?" gasped Bart when he caught his breath at last.

"I'd rather not," Adrian replied, and just then the engine rattled its last, coughed once, and locked up for good. The truck shuddered and skidded to a stop beside the highway, and the boys got out, leaving the doors hanging open to the wind. Still laughing, they stuck their thumbs in the moonlight toward Killeen.

OVER THE HILL

"Wake up, dammit!" Zip roared. "There's a friggin' river flowing through my bag. Gimme some of that poncho."

"I'm awake, you idiot," Ray seethed from the next bag upstream. "Who could sleep with you screaming your stupid head off? What, did you just notice the river? Damn heavy sleeper if I ever saw one. You've been snoring like thunder for the past hour. I swear I'd put you out of your misery if I had live ammo. And quit jerking that poncho. You've got your half."

"Shut up, assholes," growled the lieutenant from somewhere in the rainy blackness. "Whatta you boys think this is, the Holiday Inn? Just wait 'til you get to 'Nam if you think this is bad. There ain't nobody shootin' at you, is there? Anyhow, it's six hundred hours. Time to roll out of the fartsacks, boys."

It was Trueworthy, a six-month wonder just out of Officer Candidate School. He wasn't much more than twenty, and had probably never been out of Georgia before he joined the Army, much less to Vietnam. Whatever he learned in OCS besides how to be a prick, he sure as hell hadn't learned to read a map or a compass, which was why his platoon had spent the hours since midnight lost in a pathless forest, shivering in the mud in a cold November rain instead of bivouacked in warm, dry tents. Trueworthy was also lucky nobody had live bullets.

Ray crawled out of his bag and straightened his cramped back. Exhausted and cold as he was, it was somehow better standing in the steady rain than lying in it. All around him shivering shapes were emerging from the soggy lumps strewn randomly among the pines. Zip struggled out of his bag too and began to wring the water out. He was a short pudgy Italian from Brooklyn, usually good-humored. But Zip was riled. He denounced the rain as if specially provided by the Army. He swore at God and he screamed at his friends. But most of all, Zip blasted the lieutenant. Trueworthy pretended not to hear.

When they had wrung enough water from their gear to reduce it to twice the usual forty pounds, Ray and Zip rolled everything up, pulled on their soggy boots, and had breakfast. Ray had a can of apricots, and Zip opened a can of delicious green c-ration eggs, an indulgence suitable only as an alternative to starvation. Zip took one bite, spewed the curdled eggs with a curse, and hurled the opened can into the darkness. He collapsed in the mud, coughing and gasping for air. "Shit, I'm burnin' up!" he wailed.

The first light was just visible in the east when the platoon began to march, sloshing into slanting rain. The brilliant leader finally made radio contact, and concluded that they were only two miles off course. The mission was to attack base camp at dawn, still several miles away. If anybody in the platoon, with the likely exception of the lieutenant, cared whether they fulfilled their mission, it wasn't apparent. The only thing on Ray's mind was that this was the last week of basic. In three days he'd be leaving this New Jersey hellhole, hopefully never to return. And then there was the weekend pass. He closed his eyes as he slogged along, imagining a dry hotel bed, a big juicy steak, a cold beer, and no Lieutenant Trueworthy.

It had been a long eight weeks. Ray had learned a lot in those two months, more than in any year of college for sure. He'd learned to be an efficient killer, though he hadn't acquired the desire, except for maybe a lieutenant and a drill sergeant or two. He'd learned several games of psychological survival, like sleeping standing up. But most important, he'd concluded that the propaganda about being in Vietnam to make the rice paddies safe for democracy was bullshit. That became clear to him the night he spent on charge-of-quarters duty with Sergeant Grislom, who passed the hours with gleeful tales of rubbing out "gooks," descriptions of mangled bodies, methods of torture and execution and body counts.

Ray had probably been more naive than most, at least than the city boys, when Uncle Sam called. In the Oklahoma blackjacks where he grew up, most folks still believed presidents didn't lie. But at least he came armed with advice from his veteran father, which had sometimes served him well. His father's parting words: "Always stand at the center rear of the formation." That was sometimes easier said than done.

Ray's busload of recruits had pulled into Fort Dix from the Newark airport about five in the afternoon. He was assigned to the 4th Platoon, then herded off with the others to the barbershop, where their individuality was to be shorn. Expressions in the eyes of the dozen barber-school dropouts waiting behind the shears ranged from boredom to certifiable sadism. Half an hour later, styled crew cuts, full Afros, and hippie hair mingled in the dust of the barbershop floor. When they staggered out, the new soldiers all looked pretty much alike: terrible. One guy, the job half done, bolted from the chair and ran screaming out the door. He went over the hill that night and Ray never saw him again.

From the barbershop they were pushed "double-time" to supply to receive Uncle Sam's first gifts—gray plastic raincoats, field caps, and duffel bags full of belts, harnesses, packs, pouches, shovels, ammo clips, steel helmets, and dozens of other items collectively known as "field gear," total weight, about 75 pounds.

Ray especially liked his cap. "What size?" demanded the corporal of caps.

"Six and seven-eighths," he answered. The corporal handed him an eight with a sneer, and he put it on, over his ears.

"All right, scum," screamed Sergeant Grislom, a tall thick man with mad eyes and a jagged scar across his forehead, "Get those bags on your backs. You're not fit to carry the U.S. Army's gear in your hands." With gut-busting strains, most of the men managed to comply. "Down on your hands and knees you maggots!" Grislom snarled. "You're gonna learn a new mode of transportation. Now crawl, you queers. It's only half a mile to your new home, and anybody who's not there in ten minutes will find my boot lodged in his ass."

Over the gravel they crawled, balancing bags and baggy caps and perceptions of reality and illusion. "Am I the same person who got on a plane in Oklahoma City or Birmingham or Chicago this morning, or has something terrible already happened, something I haven't even begun to comprehend, much less accept?" When they arrived at the barracks at last, reality was strained backs and bloody hands and knees.

But there wasn't time to wash the cinders out. "Formation!" screeched a shrill new voice from a wiry little man Ray would come to know as his squad leader, Corporal Malona. "Get your asses outside, fairies!" the corporal howled. "You already owe me fifty push-ups for being late." So out they streamed to arrange themselves in the crooked lines of recruits not yet familiar with the sanctity the Army attaches to keeping everything straight.

In the nick of time, Ray remembered his dad's advice. Apparently, other men had received the same admonition, since there was considerable scrambling for the limited space in the center rear. They were called to "attention," which Ray soon saw had special connotations here, and introduced to their new masters—assorted corporals and sergeants, Lieutenant Trueworthy, and a snarling bulldog of a man named Bork, the first sergeant, the man really in charge of the outfit.

"All right, scumbags, listen up," Bork began. "I've got one mission in life—to make you boys so miserable you'll beg to be sent to 'Nam, just to get away from me." Then with a barbaric chuckle, he added, "I've got a few details for you rodents before chow." With that, he grabbed ten men to pick up nonexistent cigarette butts, ten to polish toilet bowls with their toothbrushes, and another handful to scrub the sidewalk. That left about a dozen men, huddling like sheep in what had been the rear, hoping Bulldog had run out of jobs.

A big smile overspread the sergeant's meaty face. "I've got just one more job," he said, dashing faint hopes. "This is a special job which requires the intellect of college boys. The Army likes to make use of its educated men, you know. I need six volunteers." From the corner of his eye, Ray saw his fellow sheep glancing distrustingly about, sniffing for a trap. He had learned a few things in college, and he sensed they were about to be had. No hands went up.

"All right," smiled the bulldog, "since you intellectual snobs are so modest, I just happen to have the names of our educated elite in this platoon. And since you'll all be taking intelligence and aptitude tests first thing in the morning, I want you college boys to be especially well prepared." He read off six names, including Zip's and Ray's. "O.K., smart boys, right after chow report to the mess sergeant for all-night K.P. Now get your stink out of my formation." So as not to play favorites Bulldog dropped the six remaining men for push-ups. It looked like a long eight weeks ahead.

Somehow Ray stumbled through the night, washing huge pots and pans, scrubbing floors and garbage cans, peeling potatoes for breakfast. By morning he knew reality was a heinous joke, and he almost didn't care. So much for inner fortitude. The Army had already won. He brightened when the PFC frying eggs asked pleasantly how he wanted his. "Over easy," Ray said. The cook stabbed the yoke with a fork.

"Watch where you're going, fool!" whined the man in front of Ray, bringing him back from his reverie. Sloshing along in mindless stupor, he had overrun the man ahead, jamming his rifle butt into the other's back.

"Sorry," Ray muttered, regaining his gait. On they trudged, too spent to talk or even curse except when somebody slipped in the mud or collided with another form in the file of zombies.

The faint glow in the east had become gray dawn without Ray's noticing, and his comrades were now defined against the trees and steady rain. Behind him Zip coughed and spat periodically. His breathing had become a pneumonia wheeze, but otherwise even he dragged on in silence. There was nothing more to say, nothing left uncursed.

About nine they topped a knoll and discovered the enemy camp arranged in a jumbled circle on a little plateau. They locked blanks in their M-16s and blazed away at clots of men huddled under ponchos. The enemy were taken by surprise all right, since they'd probably concluded that Trueworthy had lost his band so completely they'd have to be rescued. Grislom and Bulldog took turns raving at both victors and vanquished, but seeing their tirade had little effect on the walking dead, they soon retired to the headquarters tent. Ray had just enough enthusiasm left to wish he could hear what they and the company commander had to say to the fearless lieutenant.

About ten o'clock, four open semis, cattle trucks, pulled up to transport the company back to barracks. They spent the rest of the day cleaning mud out of everything they owned, and especially out of everything Uncle Sam had loaned them. There were two more days of basic. A man could stand anything for two days.

The rain even stopped, and Ray began to think he might make it. But on Friday things took a turn for the worse. It was during physical training. As they ran, the drill sergeants insisted that they chant and sing some fairly obnoxious songs. Ray could handle things like, "I don't know but I've been told, buffalo pussy's mighty cold," disgusting as it was. But what he was hating more every day was, "I wanta go to Vietnam, I wanta kill the Viet Cong." By now he was sure he didn't want to do either, so Ray didn't sing. If there was anything Bulldog didn't like, it was people who wouldn't sing with him.

"Down on your belly, reptile!" he barked, jerking Ray out of line. "Start pushing New Jersey into China." Which meant he wanted Ray to do push-ups. Ray dropped in the mud and complied with Bulldog's wishes. By now he could whip out the customary fifty without much sweat, which seemed to anger the sergeant even more. Ray was back on his feet, running again.

"Now sing, shithead," Bulldog ordered as he followed Ray around the track. But Ray didn't sing. So it was back in his favorite position in the New Jersey mud, now with Bulldog's big foot on his back, him screaming about Ray being a Commie sympathizer rather than a patriotic American boy itching to carve gook notches in his rifle stock. Bulldog's 200 pounds on Ray's back made push-ups more difficult.

So that was how Friday began. Just after noon chow the whole company gathered in formation to get their orders. Most everybody hoped to be a pencil-pusher or to work in supply, or even to assist a chaplain. But wouldn't you know it. The whole damn company was ordered to another eight weeks of infantry training, and then to Vietnam. That really made their day.

The next day was Saturday. The end of basic at last. The beginning of a weekend pass, they thought. But of course they flunked inspection Saturday morning. There was still too much of New Jersey embedded in their gear. The colonel said he'd be back in the afternoon.

After more cleaning and polishing, Ray and Zip and a couple of buddies passed the time with spitting contests and poker games, precious hours and minutes slipping away. Lots of guys had wives or girlfriends waiting, and they wondered gloomily how to break the latest bad news. Meanwhile, the life Ray had come to know in New York City went on as usual, he supposed, oblivious to his suffering.

At last the colonel returned, decided the company had been duly harassed, and turned them loose. The men were dressed in their khakis, had passes in their pockets, and were ready to pretend in various ways for thirty hours that reality did not exist. But not so fast. Old Bulldog hadn't forgotten Ray's lack of fervor for his patriotic war. "Going somewhere?" he demanded, his big hand gripping Ray's neck.

"Yes, Sergeant," Ray croaked. "I've got a pass right here," patting his breast pocket. "I'm going to the city."

"But private, you're out of uniform. You can't leave post looking like that."

"What's wrong, Sergeant?" Ray asked meekly.

"It's the buttons on your shirt, private," Bulldog said. Ray's eyes involuntarily dropped in time to see a switchblade slide down his chest, buttons popping in every direction. "Sorry, private," Bulldog smiled sweetly, "but you'll have to sew those buttons on before you leave post." Ray controlled his trembling rage—what else could he do—and went to his footlocker for a needle and thread.

Of course he missed the four o'clock bus. It was almost as dark outside as in his soul when the lights of New York came into view. Where his buddies were by now, he had no idea. But it didn't matter much. He headed for 42nd Street. The night that ensued was a blur, but Ray was warm and dry.

Next morning, Sunday, he had a splitting headache. He drank coffee and walked, to Greenwich Village, then to Battery Park to gaze at the Statue of Liberty, token of freedom for the tired and oppressed. All day he walked, eating nothing, talking to nobody. He didn't even think. No rational weighing of options, no dialectic of alternatives. There was no need to think about what you already knew.

The last bus back to Fort Dix was at ten. Ray had a cheap but delicious steak at Tad's on 42nd and headed for Port Authority. Just outside the depot he met Zip, still hacking away, a scrawny deep-eyed woman on his arm. "Ain't this the shits," Zip groaned. "One day to live and now it's back to hell."

"Yeah," Ray answered.

"I'll see you on the bus," Zip said.

Ray rode the escalator to the ticket counter. Other guys he knew were there, buying their tickets, Joe and Rich and Adrian. They'd lived their brief freedom as best they could, and now they were quiet, forlorn. "I'll save you a seat," Adrian said.

"Thanks," said Ray. He stepped to the ticket window. "Montreal," he said.

REDEMPTION

Adrian was dozing on the front porch when he heard
Morris' pickup rattling up the driveway. He'd promised Nancy
he'd mow the lawn, but she'd be gone all afternoon, so he
figured he had time for a beer and a little rest before he started.
It was Saturday, and he'd worked overtime every day for a week.
The last thing he remembered was stretching out on the porch
lounge in the sun, inhaling the fragrance of the lilacs that lined
the drive.

"Hey, Ade, look at that cloud of smoke!" Mo called from the
idling truck. "Let's go check it out."

Adrian raised up and squinted into the sun. The western
horizon was white with puffy clouds that billowed above the
horizon like thunderheads. Above the rising mounds the
cooling smoke thinned and rose toward the sun. Adrian saw
that the lilacs, the porch, even his arms had assumed an eerie
yellow tinge. He drew a deep breath. The air was spiked with
smoke.

"Wow, looks like quite a fire all right," he said. "I'd like to go,
but I have to mow the grass."

"Oh hell, you can do that later," Mo replied. "Get in and
let's go take a look."

Adrian chugged the last of the beer, which had grown warm
in the sun. He pulled on his shoes and cap and climbed into
Mo's Dodge.

"That's got to be huge," Mo said, backing down the drive. "I
wonder what it is."

"Its not the dump on fire again," Adrian replied. "It's past
the ridge, and too big anyway."

Mo headed down Cherokee and west on Highway 51. Once they passed the grain elevator they had a clearer view west. "Holy smoke. Check that out, Ade," Mo said. "That sucker is way too big to be a house. It must be either grass or woods."

"It's got to be down by the river," Adrian said. "Must be somewhere near Dawson's woods."

Mo laid on the gas pedal and they rumbled toward the smoke. The muffler leaked and the engine bellowed. He had a better truck that he used for work and family stuff, but this was his hunting rig, the one he always drove when he was in the brush or the dunes. It was old, but it took him all over the river country during quail and deer seasons.

They topped the ridge at Bradley's store, and from there the last five miles to the Cimarron came into view. It was mostly open land, except for the occasional patch of blackjacks that hadn't been cut down, and here and there a barn or some other structure that broke the monotony. "It's the river all right," Mo said. "That's a damn big fire!"

"Sure the hell is!" Adrian agreed. "I hope it's not at Dawson's. That's one heck of a nice place down there. Big woods. I used to hunt there before . . . "

"Wow, I wouldn't miss this for a case of beer, would you?" Mo said. "Lucky it's Saturday. Otherwise I'd be busting my butt at the gas plant, like I usually am when anything exciting happens."

Mo was doing seventy-five, twice what he usually demanded of the old Dodge. Adrian heard a whine he thought might be a siren, but maybe it was something under the hood, or just the wind whistling through the window wings.

Mo turned off the highway and headed south on the rutted sandy road. Blackjacks gave way to cedars and brush, and toward the river, cottonwoods. "It's down by Dawson's all right," Adrian said. "It's still at least a mile, but it seems like I already feel the heat. For sure the place is not gonna be the same, Mo. You remember that was the last place we hunted together, how long ago, twenty years? No, more like thirty."

"Sure I remember," Mo said. "That's where you got your big kill."

"Yeah, I know," Adrian said. "I'm trying to forget. I shouldn't have done it. I was just a stupid kid. After all, everything's got to eat."

"Hey, you don't need to regret it, man. That cat was wiping out the quail. Naw, you did the right thing, Ade. I just wish you'd go out hunting with me like we used to do. I really miss that, man."

"I don't know, Mo. I can't even shoot a pheasant or a squirrel any more. I keep thinking about it, how long it's been since either of us, or anybody for that matter, saw a bobcat around here. Not lately, right?"

"Don't worry about it, Ade," Mo said. "You can't really kill that sort of thing out. Coyotes, bobcats, mountain lions. Top-of-the-chain predators. They're survivors, man. They'll be back. You remember old man Stewart even claimed he saw a cougar down by the river last year."

Then they were in the smoke, and Mo laid onto the brakes. He crawled along to the intersection and turned down the river road, into the wind and out of the smoke. The wind was getting stronger, the fire sucking oxygen and the dust and smoke it bore. Ash swirled and filled the air.

"That's incredible, Ade," Mo said when they'd escaped the smoke and got the first clear view of the blaze. That's a big fire, the biggest I've ever seen! Look, it's even in the cottonwoods by the river."

"Yeah, and look how far it's already burned," Adrian said. "This stretch of timber's done for. There's no way to stop it now. I hope the old homestead didn't burn."

Weeds and grass in the ditch and the sand plums that lined the fence smoldered and smoked, and embers of brush glowed in the afternoon sun. But the universal blackness was disorienting, and Adrian didn't recognize exactly where they were until they'd passed the turnout that had to be Dawson's lane. He had avoided this road for so many years, but now he saw the grove of cottonwoods to the south and knew exactly where they were.

Mo backed up and pulled into the sandy trail. Surrounded by sand and burned-up grass, the pickup would be safe. They rolled up the windows to keep out the soot and got out for a closer look. The fire was moving north, pushed by a swelling southwest wind. Even from this distance they could hear the crackling roar when the blaze hit a cedar tree and its dry needles exploded into flame. Mo strode up the two-track lane toward the blackened forest.

"I'm not sure I want to go up there," Adrian said. "I don't think there'll be much left to see. But in fact, he was seeing too much already. He was seeing again, in the clump of plum bushes where three cottonwoods aligned, the flame-like eyes of a spotted yellow cat. The cottonwoods were towering now, twice as big as when he last was here. Their pale spring leaves, far above the undulating plain, had escaped the fire, but the plum grove was reduced to blackened twigs.

"Aw come on," Mo urged. "Let's go at least as far as the old homestead, maybe on down to the river. I want to see how much has burned." Adrian did not reply, but he trudged in silence behind his friend, his shoes kicking up sprays of sand and clouds of ash. He tried to focus on the trail, but it was impossible. His eyes were drawn to the blackened bushes, and he saw the bobcat's eyes.

He was seventeen. It was a Sunday afternoon, the few hours of freedom between church and milking cows. He got in his old Mercury and drove toward the river. There was no plan, just see what he could see. He'd hunted quail the day before, and his father's double-barreled 16-gauge sprawled across the back seat. He'd idled down the same sandy road he and Mo had just followed, turned up the same drifted lane. There were often quail here in those days, and always rabbits and squirrels. His eyes were watching for something to move.

He spotted a yellowish form, something crouched on the sandy bank amidst the leaves and fat red plums. If not for the spots he might have missed it against the tawny river sand. Could it be what he thought he saw? He slipped the Mercury into reverse and inched backward to where a break in the grass offered a better look. Big yellow eyes peered out, unblinking, fearful or fearless, he couldn't say. It was more than the spots; it was the eyes. If not for the eyes, the cat might have remained hidden behind the ragged trunk. The eyes were immense, yellow as the sun, glowing with the element of fire.

Adrian trembled at the sight. Silently he reached into the back seat and lifted the shotgun. He opened the breech and slipped in a pair of shells. He poked the barrel out the window, drew a long breath, and fired. The cat leapt, or was lifted by the blast, and fell in a silent heap.

Adrian opened the door and rushed to the thicket. The cat's mouth hung open, crimson blood seeping into the sand. The exposed eye was still wide open, penetrating his, conveying an awful indictment that Adrian could not know would require more than a lifetime to escape. He leaned the gun against the brush and dropped to the earth by the lifeless body.

What had he done? It was the only bobcat he'd ever seen in the wild, and he had destroyed it. For what? His mind raced for some justification, some threat he had cancelled, some reason that this beautiful animal lay dead at his knees. He found only shame and grief. His only desire was to deny this unpremeditated murder, to escape what he had done. He grabbed the lifeless creature by the legs and flung it into the brush where moments ago a vigorous predator had crouched. He threw his weapon in the trunk, backed to the end of the lane, and sped away.

For thirty years, Adrian had fled the accusation of those eyes. He had sought forgiveness. He had worked to expiate his guilt. But in his existential soul, he knew that he could not escape, nor should he expect to do so.

"Looks like it missed the old cabin," Mo called back from far ahead. Adrian strained to see. Through a gap in the cottonwoods he saw the sagging barn, overgrown with tumble weeds. He picked up his pace and followed Mo from the edge of the burn through the small stretch of forest that remained into familiar rolling sandhills, thick with blackjacks, cottonwoods, and sage. Half a mile ahead, the trees ended abruptly at the water's edge.

So preoccupied had he been reliving his misdeed, that when he saw the tracks he at first thought them imagined too. But no, they looked real enough. The sand was loose, so the tracks were indistinct, but they were huge. Bobcat? Adrian dropped to his knees. Slowly his mind sorted things out more rationally, and he knew that no bobcat had paws that big. There were no claw marks, so it wasn't a big dog. He ran through other possibilities and ruled them out one by one. It could be only one thing—a mountain lion.

Mo was fifty yards ahead, but when Adrian raised his eyes from the tracks to call out, he saw that beyond the forest edge and the river bank, a new pillar of clouds had appeared, not smoke, but real thunderheads. The sky was churning and dark; the sun was about to disappear. "Looks like a storm coming," Mo hollered. "Maybe we should head back." Before Adrian could answer, cottonwoods overhead began to roar and sway. The wind had shifted almost 180 degrees. In moments the sky above them was filled with smoke, and in another moment the air was dark and dense.

"Let's get out of here," Mo yelled. "The fire is coming back this way!" Adrian tried to point out the paw prints as Mo raced past him down the trail they'd come. He knew he should follow, that it was time to get out, but his knees seemed rooted to the drifted sand, his brain magnetized by the tracks. It had to be a cougar. It couldn't be anything else.

When Adrian stood up, Mo was far ahead, running hard, disappearing in the smoke. A gust of wind took Adrian's hat away, and now he felt a blast of heat. Not fifty yards to the north, a wall of flame fanned by a gale-force wind was bearing down. Adrian began to run. Then the blaze was at the trail, across the trail, and then the old barn exploded in flame. Adrian glanced behind him, and the brushy dunes were blazing too. With fire on three sides there was only south, and that was a tangle of brambles and brush. But that was his only choice. He didn't stop to calculate whether in a thicket like this he could outrun a fire driven by violent wind. Panicked, he flung himself into plum bushes and thorny vines, dodging cedars and fallen logs. Then he found a trail of some sort and plunged blindly on.

When he glanced back it seemed he'd put a little more distance between himself and the inferno, but the heat and smoke were intense. Sweat poured from his body, tears streamed from smoke-filled eyes, and he choked for breath. He scrambled on, the river now less than a quarter mile away. If he could make it to the water, he'd be OK. Then a vine caught his foot and he tumbled head over heels, landing face-first toward the fire, his nose and mouth filled with dusty sand. He struggled to his knees and crouched like a wild animal on all fours, choking on dust, coughing sand. "God, help me!" he cried.

He dragged his arm across his face, raked soot and sand from his eyes and nose and was about to launch himself back to his feet when a flash of yellow caught his eye, something crashing toward him through the brush. It was the mountain lion, leaping at full speed straight toward him, like him fleeing blindly from the blaze. In the next second, he saw in the cat's eyes that it saw him, a crumpled scrap of debris in the smoke-drenched sand. The cougar did not break its stride, but took to the air, its long lean body, stretched longer than Adrian was tall, sailing above his head so close he felt its airstream fan his face. Then Adrian was on his feet again, running blindly down the path the cougar had marked with its flight, and then the rain began to fall.

SHADOWS

"God, what a wind." Ralph fitted logs into the box, a black square against starlit snow. More than a month of winter left and the pile was getting low. February, what, the thirteenth? No, this was Friday, it must be the fourteenth. "Valentine's Day," he muttered. A good time for George to come. And clear skies meant good roads for travel. He turned his back to the wind and hoisted the wood box to his hip. "Dang fool. Should've stacked it on the porch."

He picked his way up the icy trail toward the house. A bitter gust tugged at his cap and he paused to pull it down. The porch light glowed yellow on the snow, the path to the house a dingy scar. With every step his breath came harder, and the box hunched on his thigh. "Almost there," he groaned. One foot slipped on the icy patch by the window and he nearly went down. He gasped for breath, shifted the box to the other hip, and started again. A powerful blast rattled the loose tin on the corner of the barn.

Ralph swung the box onto the porch, grasped the rail, and pulled himself up. He twisted the knob and the door screeched from his hand. He dragged the box in and slammed the door against the wind, pivoted on rubber heels and collapsed on the overshoe chair, clutching his heaving chest.

His throat felt sealed. He had to have air. He lifted himself from the chair and stumbled through the kitchen door, past the refrigerator, into the front room. He dropped like a side of beef into the armchair, which swallowed his bulk with a groan. He grabbed the oxygen mask from the lamp table and slipped the band behind his head. He gulped oxygen until gradually his eyes regained their focus.

The stove. He needed heat. One more deep breath, and he pulled the mask off. His fingers gripped the arms of the chair and he pulled himself up and shuffled back across the linoleum to the wood box.

Ralph settled again on the overshoe chair, carefully this time, and kicked off his boots. He unbuttoned the matted sheepskin and tugged at the sleeves and draped the coat on its spindle. "George's chair," he mused. "It's seen better days, like me." He fondled the rough oak edge of the seat. "Eat your carrots, George. They're good for your eyes. You'll need good eyes to see through all the lies, boy. Good eyes." He chuckled mirthlessly. He wasn't sure how well George saw things these days, but it would be good to have him home. It was something to look ahead to. Maybe tomorrow. He struggled up and lugged the wood box to his hip.

Ralph eased the box into the corner and opened the stove door. He stirred the dim coals to life, settled in a thick chunk of ash, and held his hands in the glowing mouth of the stove. Ash made a hot fire. "You know what they say, boy, nothing beats a good piece of ash." He laughed at his old joke, out loud this time. George had sure cut his share of wood. Started when he was seven or eight, worked like a man by fourteen. But he didn't work like that now, no way. And now it was money he burned. Six years in college, who ever heard of such a thing? But George knew what he was doing, even as a kid. Good education. No Viet Nam for him. Big money from the start.

Suddenly Ralph's hands were burning from the heat instead of the cold and he jerked them out. He closed the stove and lumbered back to the kitchen. "Any coffee left? Hm, just about a cup." He glanced at the clock. "Almost time for the news." He poured down to the grounds and carried his cup carefully back and flicked on the TV. A woman in a white bathing suit was eating cereal. She smiled sensuously over bulging breasts. Ralph slumped in the big chair and Dan Rather came on.

"Not that I really want to see any more of this," Ralph muttered. Last night it was the bomb shelter. A smart bomb, smart enough to find old men and women and children where they slept and turn them to cinders. What would it be tonight? His stomach felt a little sick. He reached for the knob, but hesitated. He didn't want to watch, but he couldn't turn it off. Rather was talking to a pilot, a cocksure kid who somehow reminded him of George. It was just a matter of mopping up, the pilot said.

On the screen, the gray half of a man's head turned black in the shower and a woman in just a towel grabbed him from behind. When the laughing pair faded, the screaming face of a child appeared, clutching the ruined body of a woman. "Oh, God," Ralph snorted. "There's your new world order."

He heaved himself forward and turned up the volume. "Minor collateral damage," the general pointing at a map was saying. Something about a command center. Again there was smoke, and faces, fear-blind eyes. More bodies hauled out, mangled limbs dragging in the dust. Ralph gripped the arms of the chair, his jaw clenched.

"Bastards!" he blurted at the screen. "Murder and lies! I've heard so damned many lies in my seventy-eight years I should be deaf!" Air was coming hard. He shook his fist at the screen, gasping, unable to restore the breath he'd spent. He fumbled for the mask.

Over the oxygen hum, the muffled tones of Dan Rather. Somebody said four out of five were for the war. "Mother of God," Ralph seethed into the tube, but the oxygen forced the words back to his mouth. Sweat covered his brow. He closed his eyes and exhaled, tried to expel with breath the acrid odor of burning oil, the stench of which half a century could not suppress.

A shell strikes the ammo dump and the jungle is on fire. Ralph is running through the underbrush and something crashes behind him and he plunges headlong, rifle barrel into the mud. He smears a hand across his cheek and it is covered with blood. He clutches a branch and winches himself over. From the top boughs of a mahogany tree a monkey gawks.

McCoy drags him onto his back. Three shells explode behind them, boom boom boom! They are racing through the jungle now, past torn bodies, past a man with his guts oozing out, screaming for help. Past others not screaming at all.

Ralph's hand dragged across his eyes, clawing away the scene. He knocked the mask askew, pulled it straight again and gulped air.

When he could breathe better he dragged himself forward and whacked the off knob with the back of his hand. He slid off the mask and mopped his face. He gripped the chair arms and launched himself back toward the kitchen.

In the back of the cabinet, he found a dusty bottle and poured a small glass full of whiskey. He slid the bottle back behind the shredded wheat, flipped off the light, and eased himself back to the other room. He set the glass carefully by the lamp and dragged the chair closer to the fire.

The flame reflected dimly in the window, an orange patch, and only the stars beyond. He shivered. He took a drink, and pulled the blanket from the back of the chair around his shoulders. His eyes closed again. Last month was Epiphany. Did wise men still follow stars? And what did they find?

Suddenly Ralph started. Had he dozed? No, he was awake. Something was there, in the window, an eye of flame. A face! But could it be? "Somebody there?" he croaked. Fiery eyes, but a face that he knew. The eyes drew near, crazed, full of tears, tears of blood! "The baby," he whispered. "Oh my God. The motherless child."

But no, it wasn't that child. He saw now that the face was his own! His reflection in the glass? No, it was a child's face. Then he knew the face. He twisted in the chair and gazed among the shadows. There it was on the dresser, his first photograph, masked in dust. Fifteen years after Katherine's death, still there. Ralph jerked his eyes back to the window, but there was nothing. Only the fire's glow and the stars.

Ralph reached for the glass and emptied it. He struggled to his feet and went back to the cabinet. He pulled out the bottle and twisted the cap. "You know you shouldn't do this," he said. He poured another glass and went back to his chair. The fire was dimmer now, a single tongue of flame and an amber blush. By the stars Ralph could make out the barn, the wind whipping the loosened tin. He'd have to fix that tomorrow.

The tin flapped again and flung something into the shadows. Something that moved toward him. A man? Ralph strained forward and squinted through the yellowed window pane. A tall man, avoiding the trail, glided across the snow, as if drawn by the point of flame. He wore a peaked cap. The figure turned toward the door, and Ralph saw in the profile it was a military cap. Like the other picture.

Ralph's head pivoted toward the dresser again. Whiskey sloshed out and wet his overalls leg. The face was dim, but he knew it well. It had lurked like a phantom since Ralph could first peer over the dresser. "Father!" he said.

Ralph twisted back to the window. Only the glow and the stars. He searched in the blackness by the barn. Nothing but the clamoring tin and drifting snow. He raised the glass and poured fire down his throat. Whiskey-choked, he reached for air.

When he felt better, Ralph pulled himself up and took the photograph from the dresser. Held near the stove, he saw the young man's cheeks were rosy. The nose reminded him of George. "Father," he said again. Dead someplace in France, two months before Ralph was born. They never even sent him home.

Ralph remembered the letter that told about it. It was somewhere in the top drawer still. "Funny," Ralph mused. "Seems like I knew him anyhow." Not just how he looked, but even the way he must have laughed. "The only kid in school whose father was just in his head." Ralph set the picture back with those of himself and Katherine and George. He opened the drawer and groped about for the letter, but didn't find it. It must be in a different drawer.

Though he didn't really want to, he turned the TV on again. At least there were human forms, and voices. Tomorrow, or the day after at the latest, George would be here. That would be good.

The regular news was over, but there was special coverage of the war. Ralph switched the channel to an interview with some guy he remembered from when Nixon was in. He couldn't recall the name, but he knew the big nose and the German accent. The man was explaining that you sometimes have to destroy a place to liberate it. "I think I've heard that crap before," Ralph growled. He tried the last channel. Basketball. He didn't know who was playing, but it didn't matter. He settled back and closed his eyes.

When the phone rang, he was thinking about his father again, some conversation they'd never had about rigging the harness for plowing. On the second ring, Ralph got up and went to the kitchen.

"Hi Dad. How ya doing?"

"I'm OK, I guess. Looking forward to seeing you."

"Yeah, me too Dad. But that's what I was calling about. I've got an important meeting in Denver tomorrow. A big contract on the line. The computer that guides the smart bombs. You've heard about them?"

"What's that? Bombs, you say?"

"Yeah, Dad. Production's running around the clock. So I'm afraid I can't make it up this weekend."

"Can't make it, you say? I was hoping..."

"I know, Dad. I'm sorry. But I know you'll understand. With the war going on, there's a big rush on this job. If we don't stay on top of it, we could lose the deal. There's plenty of other companies standing in line . . . "

"Did you say bombs, George?" He clung to the refrigerator like an empty locust hull. "For this war? You don't mean to say that your company . . . "

"Yeah, I know Dad, it's bad. But you know we've got to stop this madman."

"George, listen. When you didn't make it at Christmas, I was really hoping you could at least come for a weekend."

"I said I'm sorry Dad, but there's just nothing I can do. I'll get up there when I can."

"I don't know how much more of this I can take, George. This war. TV. I've got to tell you. The strangest thing. Just awhile ago I was looking out the window, and you wouldn't believe . . ."

"Dad I'm sorry, but I've got to go. I've got a lot of work to do tonight, and I've got an early plane tomorrow. Maybe I can make it up next month. Would that be OK?"

"These bombs, George. Like what they're using over there. Did you see those people they brought out tonight on TV? That baby, and the mother. But you mean to say you're in on this?" Ralph stretched the cord and dropped onto George's chair. "Listen to me, son, I've got to tell you what I saw, or at least what I thought I saw. There was this face in the window, a kid, a small body really, covered with blood."

"Look, Dad, I know those things happen. War is hell, like they say. But don't worry about it. I think we're going to come out OK. I don't think we'll lose many."

"I was thinking about my dad tonight too, George. I never knew him, you know. I . . ."

"I know Dad. I've heard the story plenty of times. But that's history now. No use going over it again. Just make you feel bad. Got to live in the present, like they say. And don't worry about this war. It'll be over soon and everything will be OK. Hey, take care of yourself, will you? Gotta go, Dad. I'll be in touch. Goodbye."

Ralph held the phone to his ear for a long moment. He hung the receiver back on the wall. He opened the refrigerator and stared blankly at the sparse items on the shelves. In the other room, the basketball game was interrupted for a special announcement from the president. Ralph hung on the door and listened. The president said negotiations were out of the question. He was ordering a ground assault to begin immediately.

"You lousy warmonger!" Ralph bawled. "You murderer. It was you killed my father, too, you bastard. Then you went for me, and now you've got my son. What else do you want?" He slammed the refrigerator door. He lunged toward the voice and his knee buckled and he crumpled to the floor. Gasping for air, he dragged himself up and staggered to the TV. He steadied himself and bumped the knob with his knee. He collapsed in the chair and grabbed the mask. His aching lungs sucked in wind.

After a time the heaving stopped, and Ralph breathed on, gazing into the void beyond the stars. He inhaled deliberately, again and again. A solitary tumbleweed emerged from the shadow by the barn and bounced past the window on the wind, hurling some weightless, wordless message to his soul. Deliberately he lifted the mask from his face and dropped it to the floor.

Ralph shivered and was aware of the cold. He hobbled back to the kitchen and filled his glass once more. He settled back in the chair and reached for the hose connector. He stared a long moment at the gleaming brass, then twisted it free and turned the valve. First with a hiss and then a rush, oxygen escaped into the room. The coals glowed brighter for a time, and Ralph could dimly read the features of faces in the faded frames.

The fire died back to the palest glow, its reflection faint in the tarnished glass. Ralph felt the familiar tightening in his chest. He finished the whiskey and braced himself in the chair, his eyes fixed on the distant stars.

CLASS REUNION

Hadley Blaze had returned to Oklahoma at least a dozen times since graduation day, but never for the school reunion. Cruising east on Interstate 40, his mind shuffled through the deck of friends from high school days.

On graduation day, they'd sworn to stay in touch, and for a year or two, a few of them did. Adrian Watson went to college in Oklahoma City, and he and Hadley both came home for Christmas that first year. Then Adrian got drafted into the Army, and Hadley never heard from him again. Once Hadley passed an old Ford he recognized on Highway 81, and he and Rolly Hopkins pulled off and talked for five minutes and went on their ways. On another trip home, he blew a tire on the edge of Enid, and who should be fixing flats at the gas station but Bobby Cain? Then Bobby got drafted too. A couple of postcards came, one from Fort Dix, New Jersey, another from Vietnam. That was before Bobby's infantry squad got ambushed on a jungle trail, and that was that. Funny how things hadn't worked out the way Hadley had imagined they would.

He thought about others, wondered if anybody else he remembered from thirty years back would show up at the reunion. If they were anything like him, chances were slim. After that many years and a dozen addresses, it wasn't likely anybody had a better idea where he was, or whether he was even alive, than he had about them. The July sun beat down on the asphalt, and face after face shimmered in the distant mirage, people he hadn't thought about for years, even decades, some faces distinct, others dim. Like him, most of his classmates had moved on, and he realized it wasn't likely they'd be back. Now that he was nearing town, he wondered what foolish notion had brought him home.

Among the faces was one Hadley had consciously suppressed for years, a face that once had preoccupied waking moments as well as his dreams: Bernice Ryan. Even after all these years and miles, the thought of Bernice brought a tightening he hadn't expected in his throat. Nobody would have questioned that she was the most beautiful girl in his high school class. In fact, of all the women he'd known over the years, few measured up to Bernice. She was as tall as he was, a lithe but shapely figure, long downy legs, breasts that stretched her sweaters, an angelic face with cascading blonde hair, and eyes so sultry and penetrating he had never succeeded in holding her gaze.

But she was off limits to him. She was of another world. Older guys with cool cars and money in their pockets picked her up after school, or they waited after ball games until she'd shed her skimpy cheerleader costume and reappeared in tight skirts or jeans.

It wasn't that Bernice wasn't friendly. She was. And who knows? If only he had somehow mustered courage to ask, she might have gone out with him—in his clattering Plymouth four-door sedan. But that had been out of the question then. Many years and a succession of women later, Hadley now kicked himself for being such an inept clod, an insecure farm boy with just enough guts to talk to girls who, like him, lived on the fringes, girls who might be available on a Saturday night when he happened to have ten dollars, because nobody else had called.

Remembering Bernice in the almost-sheer white dress she'd worn on graduation day, the Oklahoma wind flirting with the delicate ruffle above her knees, Hadley almost missed his exit. Roads and landmarks once familiar had faded in memory as his returns became less frequent, and anyway, so much had changed, houses he thought he remembered replaced by trailers or steel barns, businesses boarded up, even whole groves of blackjacks now more acres of wheat. And if the landscape had shifted in his absence, what about people?

Strangely, that realization came almost as a shock, that the static images memory harbored might be tattered by the ravages of time, just as his own once boyish face was now deeply lined, his hair more gray than the wavy brown his classmates had know. He resisted the thought that even Bernice, that enchanting angel of his youth, might no longer remain the lovely creature still so vivid in his mind. Surely such perfection could ward off the storms of life, gales that bring ruin to buildings and landscapes and to less noble women and men.

But the spell was broken. What a fool he'd been. Hadley realized that it was no more likely that Bernice would even make the reunion than that Adrian Watson would show up—or Hadley Blaze. For that matter, what if she had even joined Bobby Cain on the other side of the great divide? But worst of all, what if Bernice did appear, and what if even she had fallen from the pedestal on which she long had stood? Which would be worse, he thought, that she wouldn't be there, or that she would be, but that nothing would be the same?

Hadley touched his brake, and the T-bird glided smoothly past the city limits sign. He remembered the pink '57 'Bird that Mrs. Ortman always parked in front of the theater. Funny thing, an old woman tooling down the main street of this little farm and oil town in a car that every guy would have cut off a finger to own. If he'd had a car like that in those days, asking Bernice to go for a ride would have been a piece of cake.

The new Thunderbirds might lack the jazz of the originals, but they made up for it in elegance, plush seats, everything automatic, the cool but sophisticated car for a successful man of middle age. He wondered what Adrian would be driving if he came. Likely some battered pickup truck. He wondered whether anybody else from this hick town had gotten as far as Chicago and Los Angeles. Would he get the prize for coming the longest way?

Neither was it likely that any of his classmates had made the money Hadley had. He'd earned every penny, too, long years of hard work. There had been prices to pay, a colossal business failure before he finally got it right, two divorces, a long period of excessive drinking, too much moving around to call any place home.

Hadley pulled off at the one motel in town, the Sunset, and got a room. It was just four o'clock and the dinner was at seven, so he had time to kill. He flipped through the channels on TV, but as usual there was nothing to watch. He stretched out on the creaky bed, and thought again about Bernice. But the mirage of the highway had yielded to a dingy motel ceiling, and to more rational thought. He had to shake the stupid notion that somehow Bernice was going to walk into the room in that fringed white dress, that long blonde tresses would still frame a lovely girlish face, that she might somehow be available after all these years.

He rose, gazed soberly at the middle-aged fool in the mirror, knocked off a day's growth of whiskers, put on a clean shirt and went out. The sun was lower now, but the day still hot. Still a couple of hours to go.

Hadley cruised down Main Street. It was the same red dust-stained street he and his friends used to drag on Saturday nights, from the Sooner Grill on the north to the high school on the south, loop through the parking lot, rev the motor to make the glass packs talk, shoot the breeze and eye the girls, then do it all again. But besides the geography, most everything seemed changed. Not only Mrs. Ortman's '57, but the theater itself was gone. There were other gaps, like missing teeth in an aged mouth. No question what happened to the drugstore. The brick walls on either side were black with soot. The hardware was an exercise place where a pudgy woman pumped away on a stationary bike. The grocery was a junk store with a homemade sign that said "Antiques." The darkness behind other storefronts was softened by a heavy coat of dust.

He had passed the school before he realized it was not just shabby; it was abandoned. Then he remembered the invitation had mentioned the new school gym on the east side of town. He circled around the old brick building and stopped in the vacant lot he remembered as the baseball diamond. The bleachers were gone, but the backstop remained. Sighting past the slight rise of the pitcher's mound he found what would have been second base. He strolled to the spot he once so coveted and occasionally occupied, picked up a rock and zinged it home. A slight breeze whispered across the field, bouncing a lazy Wal-Mart bag.

Five thirty. Still time to kill. He couldn't think of anybody to visit. The people he'd known were likely gone or dead. Then he realized how thirsty he was, not just for liquid on a hot July afternoon, but for beer. For five years now his drinking had been under control; he'd finally learned when to stop, and could enjoy one or two. He remembered Friendly's Tavern.

Three pickups and an oil well service truck stood out front. The gaping depression in the brick sidewalk had been crudely filled with cement. The door squeaked open and he sauntered into the cool and smoky dark. Half a dozen faces turned to inspect the stranger, then conversations resumed. The jukebox played Merle Haggard. Some things hadn't changed.

Hadley stepped toward the bar. A slender woman in a flowered sundress faced the wall, pouring a drink. Disheveled, gray-streaked hair fell loosely down her shoulders. She set the drink before a paunchy guy in a Harley-Davidson t-shirt and turned to Hadley.

"What can I get you?" she asked. It was Bernice.

"Give me a beer," Hadley stammered, "whatever you have on tap." He slid onto a barstool, as much for support as by habit, and reached for his wallet.

Bernice drew the beer and set it on the bar with a rough red hand, a wave of foam cascading down to the blackened wood. "Say, you look familiar," she said. "You aren't from around here, are you?"

"Don't you remember me, Bernice?" he said, his voice sounding like somebody he didn't know. "I'm Hadley Blaze. I'm back for the reunion."

"Oh, yeah, sure I remember you Hadley," Bernice said. "You lived on a farm somewhere west of town, didn't you? So where you been keeping yourself?"

Hadley mentioned California, and took a long sip of beer that cleared his throat. "It's my first time back in a while."

"Yeah, I remember you, of course," Bernice said again. "You was the guy that dumped the dead skunk outside the classroom window on Halloween!"

"Yeah, I guess that was me," Hadley said with an uncomfortable chuckle. "I wish I could be remembered for something a little more—elegant. But I certainly remember you, Bernice. I've thought about you plenty of times over the years." He thought he saw a familiar flirty flicker in those alluring eyes, but it didn't last.

"California, huh?" she said. "So you actually escaped this place, and stayed gone. Lots have tried it, but most eventually came back. I even tried it myself once, but, well, it didn't work out. I suppose there'll be others you remember at the reunion."

Hadley took another sip, and his eyes slid down Bernice's still-attractive body. Still shapely, not quite like he remembered, but nice. The cotton dress still bulged in front, and the top button was open. "Maybe," he said. "I don't remember many people anymore. Are you going?"

"I can't," Bernice said. "I've got to run this dump. Roger's gone off fishing with his buddies. Who knows when he'll be back, and anyway, who cares?"

"Who's Roger, the boss?"

Bernice's laugh rattled in her throat. "I guess you could say that. He's my old man. But yeah, he's the boss all right."

"Wait a minute," Hadley said. "You mean you're married to him and he's off with his buddies so you can't even go to your own class reunion?"

"It doesn't really matter anymore," she said. "That's just the way things are."

"No, I can't believe it," Hadley said. "You, the most beautiful girl in the class, stuck in this—this bar, and you can't even get away for the night?" Hadley could hardly believe the words that had come from his mouth. He'd actually called her beautiful to her face. Why couldn't he have done that thirty years ago?

"Yeah, well, that was a long time ago, Hadley," she said. "We're not in high school anymore, and no, I'm not the prettiest girl in the class or anywhere else, and even if I ever was, you can see how far it got me." In the dim tavern light, Hadley saw only pain and bitterness in Bernice's eyes, not joking or joy, and maybe not even pleasure at his remark.

"Hey, Bernice," he said, "I haven't seen you in decades, but I still remember exactly how you looked on graduation day. I remember the white dress you wore. Listen. I've been all over the country since that day. I've known lots of women, but I've never met anybody that made me feel like you did back then. And you know what, Bernice, you're still the prettiest girl in the class."

Bernice laughed again, and it wasn't entirely bitter this time. "Well, I'm glad you think so, Hadley. It's awfully nice of you to say so."

"Hey, Bernice," yelled a guy at the corner table, "get your ass in gear and bring us a couple more beers, will you?"

"Sure, Harvey, coming right up," she said. She turned to the refrigerator door.

When she was back, the flash Hadley thought he'd seen in her eyes was gone. She busied herself with a rag, wiping down the bar. "You'd better get going or you'll miss the reunion," she said, not even glancing Hadley's way. "It's almost seven. After all, you came all the way from California for this."

Yes, he'd come all the way from California, but for what? The whole idea now seemed so absurd. He was pretty sure there wouldn't be anybody there he really wanted to see, and after all this time, nobody was expecting him. He wouldn't have been that hard to forget.

"I think I'll let it go," Hadley said. "It was a dumb idea to begin with. Now that I think about it, Bernice, you're the only one I really wanted to see." He lowered his voice. "Let's get out of here, Bernice, you and me, out of this crummy bar, out of this town. Will you go with me?"

"You must be out of your mind, Hadley," she said, too loud. "I can't just go off and leave this place." Everybody looked up from their beers, and her voice dropped to a hoarse whisper. "Roger would kill me! I tried to leave once before, and it wasn't pretty. Anyway, he'll probably walk through that door any minute now. You'd better just go. Go to the reunion. Go back to California. But don't hang around here messing with my lousy life."

As if on cue, the door screeched open. A man whose bulk filled its frame stepped through and shuffled toward the bar. He smelled of sweat and fish. "It's hot as hell out there," he boomed. "You've got it made here in this air conditioning, Bernice. Ain't she lucky?" he said to Hadley, punching his arm. "Hey, you must be the guy from California. I saw your tag."

"Oh, yeah, she's lucky all right," Hadley said, his eyes on Bernice. "It's just a question of what kind of luck." Somewhere in the recesses of memory, a dim image of Roger came into view, the football player a couple of years older than them who got kicked out of school for something; what, he couldn't recall. Roger's hairy paunch protruded from the gap between a holey t-shirt and his belt. His face was grimy with a three-day beard.

"I hope you got the back room cleaned up like I told you," Roger said to Bernice. "Hey, give me a beer."

Bernice didn't answer. She pulled a Coors from the fridge and set it in front of Roger. He twisted the top off and took a long swig. "So how about the back room?"

"You can clean it yourself," Bernice growled. "I've been busy all afternoon while you were out getting drunk."

"Watch how you talk to me, little lady," Roger said. He grabbed her arm and gripped it tight. "Soon as I finish this beer, I'll take over the bar and you can get your butt back there and finish your job."

"Hey, let go of her arm," Hadley said. "If you want the dump cleaned up, do it yourself. You don't seem overworked."

Roger slid off his stool and faced Hadley. "Who the hell do you think you are, telling me what to do?" he said. "Where did this bozo come from?" he demanded of Bernice. "One more remark from you and I'll personally throw your ass out," he told Hadley. There was a general shuffle in the recesses of the dim bar, men straightening up from slouching chairs, hoping for some action to break the monotony of the afternoon.

"You're not throwing anybody out," Hadley said. "But I'm going, and I'm taking Bernice with me."

"The hell you are," Roger yelled. His fist plowed into Hadley's jaw, knocking him off his stool. Then there were three on him, kicking and punching and dragging him toward the door.

Hadley landed face down beside the curb. He tasted blood. He dragged himself to his feet and brushed red dust off his crisp white shirt. He opened the T-bird door and slumped behind the wheel.

Friendly's door flew open again, and Bernice came through. She opened the passenger door, glanced once back toward the bar, and slid her shapely bottom into the supple leather seat. Hadley started the engine and backed into the street. Bernice's jaw was set. She stared straight ahead through the bug-spattered glass.

Jerry Wilson was born in Okeene, Oklahoma, near the Cheyenne-Arapaho land his great-grandfathers took in the Run of 1892. As a child he roamed the blackjack country of his parents' 50-acre farm east of Oklahoma City. He earned pocket money riding the roads for returnable bottles, selling watermelons at a roadside stand and trapping gophers and possums. In fourth grade his family returned to Cimarron River country, where he attended a country school, milked cows and worked in the oil field.

Jerry served a two-year sentence in the US Army, and to everybody's surprise, eventually acquired college degrees in Shawnee, Edmond and Norman, the last a PhD at the University of Oklahoma. There he married poet and fellow student, Norma Clark. After an undistinguished year teaching at a college in Altus, they ate their chickens, gave away their goat and moved to South Dakota, where with help from friends they built a geo-solar house on the prairie, raised two kids, Walter and Laura, and taught literature and writing.

Never good at holding his tongue in the face of tyranny, Jerry irritated a college president, and his teaching career went up in flames. As a recovering academic he worked as a newspaper reporter and then as managing editor of *South Dakota Magazine*. In semi-retirement he nurtures prairie, watches birds, serves as a county commissioner and writes when it's too hot or cold to play outside.

His prior publications include over 100 journal articles and magazine stories and two books. For *American Artery: A Pan American Journey*, he traveled the 5,000-mile Pan American Highway from Canada to Panama in a 1980 Dodge Omni and talked with people in every town along the way, including Okies living along US Highway 81. The second book, *Waiting for Coyote's Call: An Eco-memoir from the Missouri River Bluff*, emerged from rambles in his South Dakota prairie and woods. Between bird sightings and prairie tasks, the irrepressible characters and gritty images of three decades of Oklahoma life sometimes surface, and some wormed their way into *Blackjacks and Blue Devils*.